GW00599263

THE CHILDREN OF THE POOL

MR. ARTHUR MACHEN.

Arthur Machen in the Vorticist style, pictured in
The New Age, August 21, 1913.

THE CHILDREN OF THE POOL

Arthur Machen

Tartarus Press

The Children of the Pool
by Arthur Machen

The Children of the Pool was first published by
Hutchinson & Co. (London), 1936

This Tartarus Press printing is published 2015 at
Coverley House, Carlton-in-Coverdale,
Leyburn, North Yorkshire, DL8 4AY. UK

ISBN 978-1-905784-76-9

Printed and bound in Great Britain by
TJ International Ltd, Padstow, Cornwall

Contents

Introduction
by Mark Valentine . . . 1

The Exalted Omega . . . 19
The Children of the Pool . . . 51
The Bright Boy . . . 80
The Tree of Life . . . 125
Out of the Picture . . . 153
Change . . . 191

Introduction

Mark Valentine

ARTHUR MACHEN was seventy-three years old when he wrote the six stories in *The Children of the Pool* in the spring of 1936. They were to prove his last work of fiction. He was living in semi-retirement in Lynwood, a house in the High Street of the Buckinghamshire town of Old Amersham, in the Chiltern Hills, with his wife Purefoy. The revival of interest in his work in the 1920s, led by American champions such as Vincent Starrett, Paul Jordan-Smith and James Branch Cabell, which had resulted in new editions of many of his books, had by now lost its first fierce fire.

But he was by no means wholly forgotten, and at Amersham he still received a stream of visitors who admired his writing and enjoyed his company, and old friends from his various careers in literature, the theatre and journalism. These included Frank Baker, later to delight readers with *Miss Hargreaves* (1940), his story of a poet invented by two bored young men on holiday, who then turns up at their home town; and Oliver Stonor,

1

already a novelist and man-of-letters, who had published at Machen's recommendation a version of the seventeenth-century French canon Beroalde de Verville's *Le Moyen de Parvenir* (as *The Way to Succeed*, 1930)—a work Machen himself had also translated and which he described as a 'cathedral constructed entirely of gargoyles'.

Edwin Greenwood, actor, film-maker, scriptwriter and the author of lively, irreverent detective novels was another regular visitor; as was Colin Summerford, former monk, once proprietor of the liturgical publishers Cope & Fenwick, and his partner Sidney Duncan. Machen's niece Sylvia Townsend Warner, herself making her way in literature, and already the acclaimed author of *Lolly Wil-lowes* (1926), her novel of an independent woman finding her identity through witchcraft, was also often seen at Lynwood.

An excellent evocation of Machen in Amersham at about this time appeared in that mysterious book *Peterley Harvest* (1960) by 'David Peterley'. It is written pseudo-nymously in the form of a semi-fictional journal, but Janet Machen, his daughter, confirmed this part of the book recalled a real occasion. The journal entry is dated 23rd September 1935. The narrator visits Machen in the company of Sylvia Townsend Warner and they make their way 'upstairs to Machen's sitting-room for the first libation of his secret punch which he pours into a goblet from a huge earthenware pitcher. It is at first taste the most innocent seeming, the least apparently alcoholic, the mildest of beverages—left over, surely, from a Church bazaar.

Introduction

. . . You drink more deeply. The round countenance of Machen smiles and he says disarmingly, "A private blend of my own," and refills your glass . . . you will not rejoin yourself and the ordinary world for twenty four hours.'

Peterley gives a physical description of his host: 'He is fashioned on the lines of the oblate spheroid and would look like a Confucian sage if he did not look exactly like a Welsh wizard, which he is. The smile and white locks of Lloyd George are a mediocre imitation: for the politician is wholly of the present world, but Machen quite beyond it.' The two discuss Mithraism, and the persistence of folk memories. His visit is at the time of the town's noisy and rather riotous annual street fair and Peterley writes: 'When I reached the little upper room and saw our host pouring his punch, I had the impression of a necromancer who had conjured up the unnatural scene outside; and thought that at any moment he might put down his jug and leaning out of the window utter the cabalistic word at which the noise and the carnival would become moonlight in an empty street.' He concludes: 'He seemed a literary creation by Machen. The man is the quintessence of his works.'

The lethal effect of Machen's ladles of his famous punch becomes clear when the narrator wakes up in unexpected company in London the next day, with little idea how he got there. 'Machen's party,' he wrote 'seemed a shadowy fantastic rite performed in the light of torches to the clash of cymbals and the shouts of Bacchantes, a long way off in time and space.'

Machen enjoyed offering generous hospitality to his visitors, even though, after writing for over fifty years, he was not particularly well off: indeed he was, as he said himself, 'a man of very narrow means'. He therefore continued to look for opportunities to have old or new work published. A few years later, in 1943, an appeal fund organised by Colin Summerford and signed by many literary luminaries, such as John Masefield, T.S. Eliot, Walter de la Mare and Siegfried Sassoon raised a substantial enough sum to allow the Machens to live in a measure of comfort in their final years.

But in the period before then, Machen was also assisted by the poet, bibliographer, anthologist and busy bibliophile John Gawsworth (the pen-name of Terence Ian Fytton Armstrong, 1912-1970). Gawsworth, though then still in his early twenties, seemed to have an uncanny knack of persuading publishers to agree to his many projects. It would be fair to say that he 'collected' writers, especially neglected ones, as well as their books, and he gave practical help to quite a number when their reputations and earnings were low. He became a particular and persistent champion of Machen, and at this time was also writing a biography of him, which foundered when Rich & Cowan, the publisher who paid for it, went bankrupt. It was not published until 2005, as *The Life of Arthur Machen*, edited by Roger Dobson.

In Machen's case, Gawsworth had already persuaded Rich & Cowan to issue a selection mostly of his earlier work, *The Cosy Room and Other Stories* in 1936. Though this included one newly written piece, the fine enigmatic story 'N', Machen was embarrassed by this need to resurrect work he did not think much of, telling his old friend the occult scholar A.E. Waite in a letter of 11th April, 1936 that Gawsworth 'dug and scraped in old literary dustbins, got the stuff typed, discovered the agent, who found the publisher.' He was blunter in writing to Colin Summerford about the book on 3rd March 1936, his birthday: 'There are things in it, dating from 1890, that make me sick to look at' (quotations from Machen's *Selected Letters*, edited by Roger Dobson, Godfrey Brangham and R.A. Gilbert, 1988).

Nevertheless, it was because of this publication that he wrote *The Children of the Pool*. 'Spurred by this fine example of Armstrong's [Gawsworth], I have entered into a contract with Hutchinson to produce, by the end of July, a collection of short stories amounting to 50,000 words. I have already done 10,000 of them. I am sure that, in the words of Dryden (more or less) you will not, from the dregs of Art, think to receive what the first sprightly running could not give.'

Machen's typically modest comment about the new book was of course made before he had written most of it, and his later estimation, as we shall see, was rather more positive. He had recently provided an introduction to a lively study from the same imprint, *Witches and Warlocks* (1935) by Philip Sergeant, who had been a pupil of his when he briefly made a living from tutoring in his early days in London. Possibly this had led to the agreement to take new fiction from him.

Perhaps because commentators have taken Machen's early estimate of these stories at his own value, there has not been very much discussion of them. Of course, they are bound to seem twilight work, writings of the dusk after Machen's much-praised story collection *The House of Souls* (1906) or his masterpiece, the spiritual autobiography *The Hill of Dreams* (1907). It is probably fair to say they do not aspire to the same lyrical beauty and incantatory prose of these works, and naturally do not have the fervour and fierceness of this younger fiction. But even so the stories in *The Children of the Pool* have different qualities of their own, and show a writer still alert to the singular, fascinated by the strange, drawn to the byways of folklore and myth, and to the furthest reaches of that unknown world, the human mind. They are worth our attention.

All his life Machen held to the idea that the visible world is only a façade, a symbol of a far greater and stranger world beyond. That accounted, he thought, for the sense of mystery that some places possess: at these, the veil is thinner and it is possible to glimpse a different domain. He had recently explored this in the story 'N', in which one of his characters wanders into a marvellous garden in Stoke Newington. But when he tells his friends of this they are certain there is not, nor ever was, any such pleasaunce in the London suburb. It becomes apparent it is no earthly realm: 'I believe there is a perichoresis, an interpenetration.' his narrator proposes, 'It is possible, indeed, that we three are now sitting among desolate rocks, by bitter streams. . . . And with what companions?'

A similar theme, though with a more implied wandering into another world, is found in another 1930s story by Machen, 'Opening the Door', in which the liturgical scholar Secretan Jones walks through his garden gate and disappears for several days. On his return he cannot tell of what he has seen, but is clearly affected by it. Before he disappears in the Black Mountains, never to be seen again, he sends a letter to the narrator containing the single line *Est enim magnum chaos*, translated as 'For there is a great void' or 'a great gulf'.

Machen himself had known experiences which seemed to hint at an intermingling of this world and another during the period 1899-1901, in the aftermath of the death of his first wife Amy. As John Gawsworth recounted in his biography: 'Simply, he realised that incredible things were happening, that symbolical signs were being manifested to him, signs which he could not make out. What could a man do but distrust his senses when great gusts of incense were blow into his nostrils, and the odours of rare gums fumed about him, in Holborn, in Claremont Square, in Clerkenwell . . . And again, on a bright keen morning in November, when walking up Rosebery Avenue to become aware suddenly of a strange but delicious sensation . . . of 'walking on air', with the pavement resilient, the impact of the feet upon it buoyant . . .'

These mystic experiences culminated in a vision in his rooms in Gray's Inn when, as he wrote in *Things Near and Far* (1923), the second volume of his autobiography, 'the wall trembled and the pictures on the wall shook and shivered before my eyes, as if a sudden wind had blown into the room,' though the day was still. He tried again to explain what he meant: the wall and the pictures 'trembled, dilated, became misty in their outlines; seemed on the point of disappearing altogether, and then shuddered and contracted back again into their proper form and solidity.' Following this experience he entered 'a peace of the spirit that was quite ineffable . . . a rapture of delight' in which everything he touched 'carried with it, mysteriously and wonderfully, the message of a secret and interior joy.'

This vision is clearly recalled in the first story in this collection, 'The Exalted Omega'. The protagonist lives, like Machen, in rooms in Gray's Inn Square and is in dejection, remembering happier days. In his case, it is not the walls and pictures that shimmer, but the table, chairs and bookcases that seem not quite fixed in their place. But thereafter the story takes a darker turn as his characters hears harsh voices and the mutterings of a plot. Machen takes the opportunity to reflect upon Spiritualism. He had previously reflected on the banality of the messages supposedly received from the beyond, and written quite pungently of the credulity of those involved in the movement, including Sir Arthur Conan Doyle. In this story he also makes clear that many of its manifesta-

Introduction

tions are parlour tricks or frauds. But, unlike many other stern critics, he is willing to concede that even amongst the charlatans there are some incidents that remain inexplicable, and some did indeed seem to have unusual powers. Those powers, of prophecy, and of picking up on things happening at a distance, in a different time and place, are what drive the story, which in fact turns out to include a carefully contrived and structured murder plot.

That element of the story, artful enough, is not, however, perhaps its main allure. The reader today is more likely to relish the sense of strange conspiracy Machen weaves, and the story of the lonely bookman Mansel who makes the mark in his books that gives the story its title, a glyph like a crowned trident, the Omega Exalted. How we should like to find copies of his books with that sigil on the front endpapers, perhaps in the successors to the 'threepenny and sixpenny boxes' in the 'smaller shops and poor neighbourhoods' where Machen says his volumes probably ended up! And perhaps even the very book he names among Mansel's library, the otherwise unknown *Secret Counsels of A Certain Exile*. And yet—perhaps not. It might not be wise. For Machen leaves satisfyingly dark precisely what part the mark played in the sinister outcome of his story.

The title story in this collection also has its setting in an old haunt of Machen's, but this time in the country of his youth, in the Welsh borderlands. He rejoices again in the deep lanes, secret valleys and little wandering streams of Gwent.

9

The Children of the Pool

Machen explores the links between landscape and mood, and the black, stagnant pool of the title proves to be a potent symbol for the unconscious. The victim in the story, harried as he thinks by a girl crying out his past misdeeds, is suffering from the creations of his own tormented mind. Using the same term he had invoked in 'Opening the Door', Machen comments that 'In him, as in many men, there was a great gulf fixed between the hidden and the open consciousness. . . .' But this psychological explanation is not all that is at work. The dank pool itself played its part: the old stories about its progeny, the children, must have had some origin.

In this element of the story, Machen was no doubt drawing upon authentic folklore he had heard. His country was blessed with many hundreds of holy wells, associated with the saints and miracles of healing. But there were also tales of the reverse of these, dark waters with an unholier reputation. Francis Jones, in his study *The Holy Wells of Wales* (1954) gives a striking example: 'When Ffynnon Chwerthin in boggy land near Llanberis (Caern[arvonshire]) is approached the ground tremor causes the well to bubble or to "laugh". People attributed this to witches and their servitors, the "old black men" (*hen fechgyn duon*), and avoided it as a sinister well'. He also recounts a peculiar game played by children in the Taf valley on the Pembrokeshire-Carmarthenshire border called 'Bwci'r ffynnon' ('goblin of the well'), a hiding and chasing game in which children pretended to take away limbs and features from a child with covered eyes, who counted to fifty. When the total was reached, the child had to seek out those who had taken away his body.

'The Bright Boy' is a story that begins in an atmosphere of genteel decay, such as Machen had himself known when his father, the last of a line of priests and scholars, fell into poverty. The decline of old towns and country seats, and of obscure colleges, is sketched in at the beginning of the tale. Machen proceeds with a deft touch to hint at the lives of those not destined for great office or wealth, minor characters indeed, like the old actor in the story, based no doubt on many Machen had met in his own acting days, who is 'reliable in the smaller Shakespearean parts'. Here we see a different, more reflective Machen exhibiting a gentle interest in the broad stream of humanity, rather than the singular connoisseurs and flaneurs of his outré tales of the 1890s.

But the main scene of the story is set in Machen's Gwent, indeed in a place he had used before. The White House, as he names it here, 'terraced on a hillside, high above a grey and silver river winding in esses through a lonely, lovely valley' is Bertholly, a remote manor whose pale walls he could see from his childhood home in the rectory at Llandewi, near Caerleon. He made it the scene of the sinister experiment in his occult romance *The Great God Pan* (1894). The solution to the mystery of the child prodigy that the tutor in 'The Bright Boy' is engaged to teach is ingenious, perhaps rather too much so, and takes us again into the realms of twisted psychology.

The Children of the Pool

In his memoirs, Machen writes evocatively of his days as a lonely, bookish young man in rural Gwent in the 1870s and 1880s. They tell us much of the country, the families, the conventions and the eccentricities of this lost domain. The old armigerous squires in their low-beamed stone houses, full of character and uncertain temperament, preservers of obscure feuds and ancient loyalties, are respectfully portrayed. Machen forgives them their peppery remarks upon his wayward choice of writing as a career: and he is at pains to show that amongst all this bluster there were also signs of high courtesy and unexpected generosity. It is just these last qualities that he celebrates in 'The Tree of Life'. We think we are witnessing the increasingly peculiar orders given by a young gentleman of this sort of lineage to his steward, but soon discover that all is not as it seems. The story is a gentle tribute to the finer qualities of the families of his country, in some ways the slightest of the six gathered here, but with its own subtle strangeness.

'The Tree of Life' is a kabbalistic term for a diagram of the spiritual spheres. This concept is not in fact explored in the story of that title. But Machen certainly had in mind a kabbalistic theme in his next story 'Out of the Picture', as is clear from a query he put to Waite in the letter quoted earlier: 'And since we are discoursing of interior things,' he wrote, 'tell me if I am right in declaring that the Serpent did not ascend beyond Daath (the logical understanding) in the Tree of Life? And furthermore; that being so, we may speak of the world of

Introduction

Kether, & the works of it as uncorrupted? Or, in terms of literature, may it justly be said that Pope's Character of Addison is of Daath, while Coleridge's Kubla Khan is of Kether?'

He added: 'All this, let me tell you, relates to a mystical painter of mine in a 50,000 word collection of stories, commissioned by your pal Hutchinson'. The publisher was Waite's 'pal' because he had agreed to publish the occult scholar's extensive autobiography: Machen jokingly suggested to Waite that 'Walter' Hutchinson, the head of the firm, was often found sobbing over his tea as he contemplated a further large batch of the memoirs.

In 'Out of the Picture', Machen uses similar phrasing to that in his letter to Waite and explains what this means in the mystical tradition: that humanity's highest faculties were not tainted by sin, by the Fall. He is also using Kabbalistic terms to support his long-held distinction between 'literature', characterised by a sense of ecstasy, and other, supposedly more 'realistic', writing, which he regarded as something lower, less inspired. The story also includes a passage referring once more to a variation on his own experience in his Gray's Inn rooms, and still trying to find the words to convey this: 'A mystic once told me that after he had finished his meditation and gone out into the street, he had seen the grey bulk of the houses opposite suddenly melt, evaporate, go up like smoke, leaving void nothingness in their place.'

M'Calmont, the artist in the story, argues that the finest music achieves a pure form, and wonders if art can do the same. As if conscious that these discussions might seem somewhat esoteric and abstruse, Machen soon introduces a more tangible, physical horror into his story. His tale is a variation on the idea that a painting could contain a dark, supernatural secret within it, most notably explored by Oscar Wilde in *The Picture of Dorian Gray* (1891): Machen met and dined with Wilde several times in the period after this book appeared. In Machen's hands the theme is notable for the scenes set in the lonely, obscure back streets of London where the artist has his studio, and the work is a very effective drama of mounting dread.

We might wonder whether Machen had in mind an actual artist in his creation of M'Calmont. There are aspects of this character that seem to suggest Austin Osman Spare (1886-1956), the London artist who was immersed in kabbalistic magic and his own original system of sorcery. It is not known that Machen ever met Spare, but he did know well Spare's former partner in the journal *Form* (1916-17), Francis Marsden, the pseudonym of Frederick Carter. He had been introduced to him by John Gawsworth, met him several times for pub conversations, admired Carter's story 'Gold Like Glass', which the poet and editor had anthologised, and wrote an introduction to Carter's book of mystical art, *The Dragon of the Alchemists* (1926). It seems at least possible he had heard of the remarkable character and art of Spare from Carter.

Introduction

In the final story in this volume, 'Change', the setting is Pembrokeshire, which Machen had also used in a novel written in this period, *The Green Round* (1933). He and his family had taken annual holidays in this region, around the town of Tenby and the coastal village of Penally, and Machen explored the neighbouring country and discovered something of its folklore. And in this story he revisits another strong element of his past writings, when he was the chronicler of the Little People, the subterranean survivals of an ancient race, in stories such as 'The Novel of the Black Seal' and 'The Shining Pyramid'.

Starting with the mild picture of families on holiday and children playing on the beach, he soon brings us, with all his old gusto, into scenes where this darker world impinges on our own, in a macabre account of that most ancient tradition, of the changeling: the child taken by fairies, who leave one of their own in its place. In his last significant work of fiction, Machen demonstrates he has lost none of his power to convey the utterly outlandish and sinister. The final words of the story, of his book, and of his long career in the fiction of the supernatural, sum up his conviction that we live in a world that, if it sometimes offers us great wonders, is also fraught with spiritual peril: 'the darkness is undying'.

Arthur Machen's considered verdict on this book was given in a letter to A.E. Waite of 16th November 1936: 'I believe you are right in thinking that there are hints or indications of new paths in *The Children of the Pool*:— but it is getting very late & dark for treading of strange ways'. He was always a modest man, reluctant to acclaim his own work, but between the lines of this comment it is possible to see a quiet pride that he was still able to advance original ideas and pursue curious, unexpected paths of thought.

THE CHILDREN OF THE POOL

The Exalted Omega

I

ONE DARKENING autumn evening, not long ago, a man stopped a moment in his quarter-deck walk up and down his sitting-room in Gray's Inn Square and gazed out of the window at the trees, tossing and restless before the west wind, with a look of vague perplexity, in which there was a slight hint of uneasiness. Not more than a hint; it was rather the air of a man who is confronted by a minor difficulty or obstacle in some little plans he is making, or in the train of thought he is following; and to be precise, with J.F. Mansel, the personage in question, it was hardly so large a matter as that. The fact was that Mansel had been a good deal struck by an odd book he had once read, the 'Adventure' of two English ladies in the gardens of Versailles. Most people, I suppose, have read the book in question, and have puzzled their heads over it, and tried to find some plausible explanation of its story: a day in the French Revolution returning over the gulf of years; the image of the lady sketching in the garden, the lady who must have been Mary Antoinette, the hurrying

19

messengers, perturbed footmen, stolid gardeners; all, as it appeared, going about their affairs, quiet or unquiet, as they had gone about them on that October day in 1789.

But Mansel was not thinking, as he stared out of the window, of the men and women whose apparitions, as it seemed, had been called up to puzzle the two scholastic Englishwomen and their readers. For the moment, it was not the ghostly people, but the ghostly landscape of the vision—or whatever it was—that slightly troubled him. He recollected that either Miss Moberly or Miss Jourdain—or was it both ladies?—had noted at the time of the strange experience, as they walked by woods and groves that are not marked in the modern maps of Versailles, since they have long ceased to exist, that the scene had something unusual in its aspect, that the trees were more like the pictured trees in a tapestry, objects on the flat, than the stout growth of the common wood. And, as it happened, Mansel looking out of his window on that familiar scene—the plane trees of the Inn Garden, and the turf beneath, and a glimpse here and there of Raymond Buildings on the other side of the lawn—was reminded of the Versailles manifestation. There was, he hesitated, something not altogether solid and satisfactory in the sight before him. It looked, he felt, as though leafage and tree trunks, green turf and grey bricks of Raymond Buildings wavered together, as he had seen vistas and towers wavering on the theatre backcloth, in the old days when things, perhaps, were generally more cheerful, and he had been used to go to the play. He glanced again, and doubtfully supposed it was all right, because it must be all right; and then turned from the window to the fireplace, and sat down in the ugly, comfortable arm-chair, which he had brought up from his old home in the west, quite a long time ago. There was a little round table beside the chair, one of those papier mâché pieces of the 'thirties and 'forties, that people are beginning to esteem curious. It had a painting of woods, and a lake, and distant mountains on it, with an inlay of mother-of-pearl and a cusped and gilded edge. It had been in his Aunt Eleanor's drawing-room at the Garth. Aunt Eleanor's work-box usually stood on it, and obstructed the view of the painted scene, somewhat to the distress of Johnny—as they called him then. He wanted to stand by the gleaming lake, where the sunset light shone on the water through a cleft in the trees. He desired also to track a path—he saw the entrance and the beginning of it—that wound through the dark, rich wood; there to gather unknown purple flowers that drooped in the shade, and at last, perhaps, to come out and ascend the shining mountain-tops: which he called The Land that is Very Far Off.

The work-box had vanished long ago; he thought that Cousin Emma had taken it away with her after the funeral; and when Emma died thirty—or forty?—years ago, there had been a sale and everything was scattered. He rather missed the work-box now, and wished he had secured it; but Durham was a long journey. There was a book on the table, the *Secret Counsels of a Certain Exile*. He laid a hand on it to take it up, but let it stay beside the lake, and sat back in his chair, and half-dozed and half-waked, and scarcely distinguished between a broken dream and a confused waking. Outside, the September evening darkened, and the leaves stilled as the west wind sank to peace. The jangle of the 'buses, the cry of the newsboys, the traffic of Theobald's Road, sounded very faintly; now and again there was a dull thud as the last clerks to go banged the outer doors of the lawyers' offices on the stairs. The place grew heavy with the silence, and the lamps began to flicker in the square.

Mansel lay back in the soft comfort of his arm-chair. When he woke, or half-woke, he found his room dark about him, and didn't trouble to light the candles—he had never used gas or electricity in his rooms. He would soon get up and light two candles on the mantel-shelf; but, as he considered, there was nothing particular to do, and he might have supper instead of dinner; there was a 'bus that would take him from the corner of Theobald's Road down to Shaftesbury Avenue. He thought of the jolly hours when, perhaps, 'things had been more cheerful,' long ago, soon after he had come to live in the inn: great evenings at the Café de l'Europe in its golden days. Indeed; why shouldn't he go there tonight for his supper? It might be, likely enough, that he might meet Tom, or Dick, or Harry there; or, perhaps, all three of them; and the old quartet would be assembled again, and the old jokes and passwords recalled, and the band in its balcony would play the tunes from *The Belle of New York*. The recollection merged into a dream: there he was at the table in the corner, with his old friends about him, and nothing said about his long absence, and the band blared away as in the merry time. There was the question of a dream within the dream. For as he sat and talked and laughed with his friends: it suddenly struck him that, after all, it was not as it had been: there was a sad and heavy background, or a cloud that drifted across his happiness, that he had known nothing of long ago. Let go: but, what if he had dreamed all those years of heaviness, as he slept in his chair in the inn? They had never been, perhaps; he had met Tom, and Dick, and Harry last night, and he would meet them tomorrow. He shook his head, as if to drive the shadow away, and rattled the lid of his *krug*, and left it open, to show the waiter that he wanted more Munich beer. He had quite forgotten that Tom, and Dick, and Harry had been dead for years, that friendship had failed before life failed; and that the Café de l'Europe had closed its doors twenty years before.

The scene of the café had dissolved, and formless sleep had come heavily upon him, when he started up, roused by a woman's voice, raw and raucous. As he woke, he heard the words:

'Quiet? Mahvlessly quiet, I'm sure. In fact, I should call it bloody quiet.' She shrieked like a macaw.

The voice burst through his head, like an express train whirling and thundering through a station. He staggered up out of his chair, and stared, distraught, about him. For a moment, swift and gone as a flash, though he had not lit those candles after all, the room seemed glaring bright,

and all disturbed and quaking, till his chairs and tables
and bookcases shivered and settled down into their
accustomed places. They were his chairs and tables? The
garden was in moonlight; and he crept cautiously about
the room, and satisfied himself that each piece was in its
accustomed place.

Mansel had long been aware that the sharp outlines of life
and time and daily event were becoming blurred and
indistinct for him. He was apt, he knew quite well, to
confuse the years and those who passed through them. He
would assign in thought this or that friend to a year long
before the time when the two first met; he would think of
men talking together who, in fact, had never encountered; a whole group of interests were antedated or post-
dated. Edwardians wandered back into the Victorian
years and sometimes a young countryman of his boyhood
in the west would stray into the café and seem familiar
with the place and with those other men whom he had
never met, or even heard of. And, then, Mansel would
question himself: 'After all, wasn't there a night when
Vaughan joined us and came up to my rooms afterwards?
He did come up to town once, I'm sure. Or, did I dream
it all?' He was never quite sure. He felt that his lonely
habit and silent days were more and more closing in upon
him like a cloud; but by the time he had realised the
danger—if it were a danger—his resolution and will to
live clearly and in the light of the day had weakened and
dissolved. Once or twice, old friends had looked him up

and tried to rouse him and to renew laughter and life within him. But it would not do. Mansel remembered very well who they were, or rather, who they had been; for they had become strangers, or ghosts that spoke of ghostly meetings that had lost all savour. The talk would die down, the man would feel his cheerful intent sink away from him, and go as quickly as he could, and hardly summon a conventional smile as Mansel closed his outer door.

'Poor Mansel!' he might say afterwards. 'I could do nothing with him. He's not interested in anything. I tried him with the sort of talk that used to set him on fire; but no good. He might as well be dead, it seems to me.'

So, one by one, his friends dropped away and left him alone, wondering what had happened to dry up all the springs of joy. Indeed, the question was an obscure one. There had been no tragedy, no violent disappointment or loss, no specific malady of mind or body, to be ascertained, defined, and encountered with remedies. He had been conscious of a savour gradually departing from the whole body of life, so that a grave book or a gay gathering had become alike flat and meaningless. Walking up and down his rooms, laying down the law, arguing, growing heated about the essence of poetry or the demerits of Meredith: that had been fine, relishing sport once on a time: and now it was nothing. He would look at old note-books he had filled, and wonder what possessed him to write down all those futilities. And then; the last cheerful evening that he had attempted with his old friends, who drank a little and laughed a great deal; that held no cheerfulness for Mansel. He asked with Johnson: 'Where's the merriment?' and stole away home very sadly, and sat alone in the dark room. And one of these old friends talking to another, said: 'I don't know what's happened to Mansel. He may have sinned against the light or he may be suffering from some obscure form of liver. I feel sure he hasn't taken to drinking methylated.'

Mansel was a good deal vexed with that sudden shriek of a woman's voice that had made him start up from his dreams and drowsy recollections. He could not make it out. There was nobody in any one of his three rooms; he was sure of that. He found his outer door shut fast. The only other person to have a key was his laundress, and she only came in the morning. Besides; she did not talk like that. Her voice was soft and heavy and suety; and she was particular as to what she said, in the presence of her clients, at all events. The voice could not have come across the landing; where the rooms were inhabited by another lonely bachelor. It might have been somebody wandering about the place, looking for rooms, and standing on the landing itself. There was certainly that small opening contrived in the wall, by the door, to enable the tenant, summoned by a knock, to stand in the darkness and inspect his caller, displayed in the light of the window or the lamp. The raucous cry that had roused him might, perhaps, have penetrated through the hole in the wall. He hoped that no such company might come about his stairs again.

But here he was disappointed. Again and again, and constantly, his journeys into the past, and dreams and meditations were broken by a hubbub of voices, shouts of laughter, always accompanied by that glare of light in the moment of awakening, the sense of disturbance and confusion in the objects about him. He was perplexed and frightened, and wondered whether he were going mad, for it was clear that there was no ordinary explanation of the strange trouble. He thought of consulting a doctor, but he knew he could never summon up the resolution for such an encounter. And so he grew into the sense of being hemmed about by these dismal visitants, creatures, he supposed, of his own morbid fancies or diseased body. They were not real; he was sure of that. In the darkness of the night, as he came up from the wood of the purple flowers, and stood in the sunlight on a shining, happy hill—perhaps the true Land that was Very Far Off—a shriek of laughter would shatter his dreams, and he would start up in terror, and his gloomy bedroom would be ablaze.

And, then, the trouble began to beset his day-dreams in another form, without the violence of the awaking. He heard the woman, her voice subdued, though it still grated on his ears, murmuring, murmuring, and a gruff man's tones, assenting or objecting or denying. It would seem that this muffled talk went on, day after day, night after night; and by degrees Mansel got the impression that he was listening to the plot of a deadly business. There were mysterious allusions to 'a bottle party,' which conveyed nothing to him; and someone called 'Cousin Jerome' was to get a drink from the right bottle; and the man's voice, answering, it seemed, a question, said 'eighty thousand at least, perhaps more.' And, then, again the words came: 'No danger, no danger. No weed killer for me, no fly-papers, or any damn childish tricks of that sort. You have only to hang the leg of mutton long enough; and the juice of it will have no taste or smell or colour. The place will be all shut while we are away in the country. If anything gets through closed doors and windows; I daresay rats die under the floor now and then.'

And one . . . night or day, he could hardly tell which; as if the low voice were speaking in his very ear: 'Old Mansel will never tell.' And then they laughed, quite quietly for once: and those five words struck through his soul with unutterable horror.

He thought that one misty evening he must have left his rooms and wandered out of the inn to escape that instant horror that beset him. He could not tell the way he took, but he thought he remembered crossing a bridge, and straying on through unknown places, till he found himself in a maze of streets almost deserted; streets of little houses; dismal, monotonous, and yet pretentious. There was one house with a great green bush growing up from the area, and here he stopped, and somehow found himself within it. He was in a small room on the ground floor; a shabby and flashy room with flaring, foolish ornaments above the empty grate, and a gaudy linoleum on the floor. At the gimcrack table there sat a party of seven people, there were six men and a woman; three on each side; and at one end, a stout, dark, middle-aged woman, with black and greasy hair elaborately done in a sort of structure on top of her head. She wore a black and shiny and belaced dress, shabby and pretentious like all else in that place. The others bent their heads in an attitude of profound attention; the woman at the head of the table seemed to gaze before her, as if she saw nothing. She held up her hands in the Jewish attitude of prayer; and began to sway gently to and fro. The light was dim, for there was only one gas jet burning, and that was turned low, but Mansel noted big rings studded with apparent emeralds, rubies, and diamonds thick on her fingers. One of the men at the table got up and sat down again, and a gramophone began to discourse, 'Abide With Me.'

The dark woman spoke in a thick, unctuous voice:

'I get a message for Sam. Is there anyone here named Samuel?'

A man looked up eagerly, and stuttered, as he answered.

'I haven't been called Samuel since I was a nipper nine years old. My name is Albert Samuel Morton, right enough, but I always call myself Albert Morton. Who can it be?'

'I get a message for Sam. Ask him if he remembers Aunt Clara. Clara? Clara? I am not certain about this name.'

'It's not Clara,' said the man, excitedly. 'I had an Aunt Sarah, all right.'

'It comes through clearly now. Ask him if he remembers his Aunt Sarah, and her china dogs.'

'So she had!' exclaimed the man. 'On her mantelpiece in the parlour. I can remember them. It's wonderful.'

'The message says: "Look after the pence, and the pounds will look after themselves!"'

'That's Aunt Sarah, right enough!' The man bubbled with amazement and delight. 'Why, that was a regular saying of hers. My dad always called her "Saving Sarah"! Isn't it wonderful? Well, I'm glad to think she's not forgotten me.'

There were more messages of much the same character. Most of them seemed to find an echo in the breasts of those present. There was one woman who could not remember any 'Cousin Joshua,' who seemed distressed about some matter which he said she would understand. The woman reflected, and said: No. No, she couldn't recollect any Cousin Joshua.

'Perhaps,' said the lady at the head of the table, 'he died when you were very young. There may have been something painful, which prevented his friends talking about him.'

The woman's face was blank; then she started slightly, and kept silence; looking a little frightened.

There was a pause. The gramophone had run down. The dark woman had seemed to deliver her last message

30

with a certain difficulty. Her voice faltered; she paled through her paint. There was silence in the dim room.

The woman shuddered as if an electric shock had passed through her. She shook from head to foot. Her face was twisted all awry. And then she suddenly bent forward, and began to scribble with a pencil on a piece of paper that lay on the table before her. Her crooked face was all ghastly and twitching, as she rather struck with the pencil than wrote; and in a few seconds, it seemed, there was a harsh noise in her throat, and she fell sideways from her chair to the floor, in some kind of fit or seizure, that was very dreadful to behold.

The clients started in alarm from their places. Someone turned up the gas, and the two women of the party approached the epileptic fearfully. A bell was rung, and a timid, shadowy little man came running upstairs and looked into the room, a sluttish servant following on his heels. Two or three of the party carried out the dark woman, still struggling and foaming. One of those who was left picked up the paper that had fallen to the floor. He scanned it curiously under the gas, now flaring.

'You can't get much out of that,' he said, in a disappointed tone. 'A lot of marks that don't look as if they meant anything, and something about "grows my spirit," and more marks. The fit was on her, no doubt.'

He laid down the paper on the table, and turned to go.

Mansel, vague as usual, supposed he must have found his way out with the rest of the party. No doubt, he mused and wondered over the strange ending of the evening as he made his way back to the inn, and took no note of the streets through which he passed; for his next impression was of the familiar room. It was silent at first; and then he caught once more the mutter of those evil voices.

II

There can be no doubt, I am afraid, that Mrs Ladislaw sometimes cheated. Her mediumship had often been assailed, and not merely by the incredulous outsiders who take a pleasure in turning on their torches at inopportune moments, and in grasping at ectoplasm and giving it another name. Eminent Spiritualists had exposed her in their papers. It is true, that other eminent Spiritualists had at first taken her part, and had called for justice and for the spirit of English fair play. There had been the spirit paintings, for example, which were supposed to blaze out suddenly on a blank sheet of paper. It seemed alright at first. There was the paper laying white and virgin, on the table before Mrs Ladislaw; and half a dozen coloured chalks beside it. She would lay a large, fat hand upon it and the chalks, and go into a mild trance; then, the hand was lifted, and a glowing work of art appeared on the page. But an elderly and honoured Spiritualist first of all recognised the picture submitted to him as an indifferent copy of a coloured plate that had appeared in a Christmas Number many years before. There was a controversy about this in the *Metapsychical Review* and in *Daybreak*. It was pointed out that the subject matter of the picture was beside the point; the question was how had it appeared on a piece of blank paper in the course of a few seconds. How, if not through the agency of Red Bull, Mrs Ladislaw's control? This question was answered before long in a sense which seemed to make the aid of Red Bull superfluous and unnecessary. Then, there were questions on slips of paper, which were placed in a casket, and duly sealed by one of the sitters, who had brought with him an old armorial signet ring, with an elaborate coat engraved on it. At the next séance, the casket was passed round, and it was clear that the seal had not been tampered with in any way. It was then solemnly broken by the owner of the jewel; and inside the box, there were the slips of paper with the questions, and answers, more or less coherent, written beneath in scrawling, untidy script. This interesting manifestation was repeated several times and made a considerable impression. It seemed quite clear that on each occasion the seal was absolutely undisturbed; and people of some intelligence were beginning to be interested, when one of these thought of turning the mysterious casket upside down, and discovered the secret in the construction of the bottom of the box. It slid open, in response to judicious pressure on one side of the four knobs or feet on which it rested. So, on the whole, it was felt in the higher circles of Spiritualism that Mrs Ladislaw must be dropped; that she must be seen no more at the College of Research, or at the Spiritualist Institute. So she carried on her business in some obscure street in South London, and, on the whole, satisfied her local clients very well. They were not critical; they had never heard of the *Metapsychical Review*, they accepted the messages they received, and when the lights were turned quite out, they enjoyed the marvellous things that happened. None of them carried an electric torch to the dark seance; none of them raised objections if the spirit of a Roman Cardinal uttered the blessed word 'Benedictine'. So Mrs Ladislaw sank to the lower levels of necromantic culture, and was heard of no more amongst literate Spiritualists. And yet, a few who had seen her in her more prosperous days maintained that, in spite of all, there was something strange about the woman, something not altogether explicable. They confessed that she was, beyond doubt, an arrant cheat: 'there can be no doubt that Eusapia Palladino cheated, and cheated almost openly at times,' one of them reminded me, and he went on: 'Mrs Ladislaw's childish tricks don't deceive me for a moment. They were old tricks that were going in the 'sixties, as you can see if you look up the newspaper files of the time. They were exposed then, and were forgotten, and this woman, whose mother may have been in the business for anything I know, brought them up again, and ran them till they were exposed a second time. But it wasn't all cheating; not quite all. I remember sitting with her at the Institute, seven or eight years ago. It was a summer afternoon, and the seance room was in full light. There were about a dozen people there. Mrs Ladislaw was doing the

Red Bull act. She had passed round the half-sheet of note-paper that was to show the picture in a minute or two, so that everybody might see that it was absolutely blank and clean. It went round from hand to hand, and people looked at it hard, and held it up to the light, and felt the texture of the paper to be sure that it was one piece, not two. One man pulled a magnifying-glass from his pocket, and went over the surface inch by inch. Two or three were trying what they could make of the coloured chalks, turning them over, and weighing them in their hands: I don't know what they thought that would do, I am sure. I wasn't bothering about the chalks or the paper myself, you see, because I know how it is done.

'Anyhow: pretty well everybody was busy investigating and testing and the rest of it, with their eyes fixed on the table, or the paper going its round, and two or three of them were arguing in low voices about the fluidity of matter.

'You don't know Séance Room 5 at the Institute? Well, the table runs down the room between the fire-place and the window. I was sitting half-way down with my back to the fire-place. I was looking at Mrs Ladislaw, dark and greasy, who was sitting straight up with her fat hands flat on the table before her. She was doing the dignified and impassive fairly well: presently, as I knew, when those keen fellows had finished investigating, she would begin her trick.

'Her face changed. She turned her head a little, and I saw her staring at the wall behind me. She went white.

Her mouth dropped open. She was glaring with terror at something that was happening at the back of my head. Naturally, I looked round to see what had frightened the woman.

'In the middle of the mantelshelf behind me was one of those infernal Greek Temple clocks, in black and green marble, with rows of pillars and gilding where it had no business; an ugly, heavy thing. It was at this clock that Mrs Ladislaw was staring: frozen with fright. And then I saw the clock rise high from the mantelpiece and sail gently down onto the floor. Mrs Ladislaw fell forward with her face on the table, in a faint.

'The séance broke up in confusion. The women looked after Mrs Ladislaw. In the process, the picture that was to have appeared if things had gone better fluttered from somewhere onto the floor, and there was some argument as to what this proved. I got up, and looked at the clock, which was sitting on the carpet. I lifted it up—heavy goods—and put it back in its place. No; no wire, or thread, or anything of the sort, and if there had been, it wouldn't have accounted for anything. If that lumping thing had been twitched from the mantelpiece, it would have fallen with a crash. It *sailed* down, quite gently, like a feather. You can call it a Poltergeist case, if you think that makes it any clearer. I don't. I don't know how in the least it was done. But, as I was saying, I've always thought since then that there was something odd about the old swindler that she didn't understand herself. I never saw anybody look so frightened as she did.'

The Exalted Omega

It is to be assumed that this tinge of interest in 'the old swindler' led this cautious and sceptical investigator of obscure things to keep in some sort of touch with her down in the lower levels to which she had drifted. Anyhow, it was through this man, Welling, that I was made acquainted with a very queer business, in which Mrs Ladislaw played a part—a principal part perhaps it might be called, but I don't know about that.

A month or so before, Welling had sent me a singular script, an example, as he said, of what is called 'automatic writing'. A lady living in a small town in Somerset had discovered that she possessed this gift. She had sat down at her desk with pencil and paper before her, intending to make a list of goods she required from the grocer. She took the pencil in her hand, and, as she declared, it 'ran away with her,' and proceeded to scrawl and scribble away at a great rate. The slip of paper was soon exhausted, Miss Tuke supplied another, and again the pencil raced away. It had covered six or seven sheets before the impulse or whatever it is ceased. And this had happened several times when Miss Tuke communicated with my acquaintance, Welling, and asked his opinion: should she persist, or resist the impulse when it next occurred?

'I told her,' said Welling, 'to go on if she liked; provided she regarded it as a parlour game, without any consequence, and quite devoid of any sort of authority. The scripts? Oh, the usual thing: pious exclamations—I understand Miss Tuke is a Wesleyan—and moral maxims, and all sorts of vagueness, and words running into each other, and some repeated three or four times. But this last thing she sent me is a bit of a curiosity; it seems to be Latin tied into knots. I haven't time to disentangle them. But the lady assures me that she doesn't understand it, as she knows no language but her own.'

I took the slip home, and found it was much as Welling said: scraps of Latin that read as if they had been taken down from dictation by somebody ignorant of Latin. I corrected the text without much difficulty, and it gave up a number of admirable sentences that might have been extracted from the Fathers: 'Jordan was driven back that Israel might enter the land of promise: in like manner it is necessary that the river of our sins be turned back if we would come into that holy land of our inheritance': and a good deal more in that vein. How Miss Tuke came by it all, we never knew. I gathered from Welling that there was no reason to doubt her word, that she knew no Latin. He was inclined to think that she had read it all without understanding it when she was a child, and that it had been preserved, imperfectly enough, in her subconscious memory: a guess, nothing more. And soon after, Welling told me that Miss Tuke had written to him to say that she had given up her 'sittings' with pencil and paper, as she thought it was an unsuitable employment for a middle-aged woman.

And all this leads up to something much more significant; at least, so it strikes me. One day, not long ago, Welling called on me, and began at once on Miss Tuke's Latin script.

The Exalted Omega

'You know how you made sense of that stuff. Well, look here. This is worse, and I wonder whether you will be able to make anything of it. Here you are; see what you can do.' And he handed me a sheet of paper that gave the effect of a child's scribble.

'And what is one to make of that trident thing or whatever it is?' He was evidently a good deal interested. And I was more than interested when I saw the device which he had called 'that trident thing'.

It was the oddest looking document. At the head of the paper, the word 'quotient' was repeated six times. Then came 'poison' scrawled in large, loose letters. Then the word 'ore' was written twice, followed by 'or,' and then 'oar' was written three times. Then 'quite' and finally, the words, 'grows my spirit.'

It was not difficult. It was, clearly, an attempt at a familiar phrase in *Hamlet*, 'the potent poison quite o'ercrows my spirit'; written, apparently, by a person in delirium. 'Quotient' for 'potent' was odd; but there were similar mistakes in the more subdued scripts of Miss Tuke: the effect being, as I noted in some of her communications, that of a dictation taken down by somebody who failed to catch the exact sound of individual words, and had no notion of the meaning of the complete sentence.

But all this was a very minor matter. It was the symbol that I found exciting. It was dashed all over the paper, sometimes obscuring the writing. It was not exactly a trident. I should have described it as a small Greek omega, at the end of a stick. The two outer lines of the letter were curved inwardly; the middle line, which in a trident is equal in length to the others, was barely indicated. The 'stick,' as I have called it, was about an inch and a half long.

'Now,' I said to Welling, 'would you tell me about it, and where it comes from?'

'Well, it's rather queer. You remember me talking to you about that medium, Mrs Ladislaw, and the clock business?

'Well, for that reason I kept something of an eye on her doings. You know she's been down in the world some time now. She lives somewhere in Stockwell, and has séances there, and makes what she can; the old game, the old tricks. There was one of these séances a week ago; and people were getting messages from Aunt This and Uncle That, and they were satisfied, and everything was going all right, when quite suddenly, Mrs Ladislaw began to twist her face about and scribble away on this bit of paper. And then she went into a fit, and a pretty bad one. A man I know was there, and brought this along, thinking it might interest me. What do you think of it?'

I told him that, apart from the *Hamlet* quotation, there were some interesting points that I should like to go into at leisure. I promised to let him know if there were anything of real consequence involved, and so sent him on his way.

The Exalted Omega

It was the omega mark that concerned me. About twenty-five years ago, I was living in Verulam Buildings, Gray's Inn. In summer, it was often my habit to take a turn about the Square, on fine nights, after the gates were shut; and I soon became aware of a small nocturnal population, who were never seen about the inn at daytime. There were three of four—perhaps five or six—of them; and they prowled in a hapless, aimless, hesitating fashion; stopping now and then and looking vaguely about them, and then moving on, dragging one foot slowly after another. They never spoke to each other, or seemed aware of one another in any sort of way. It is a race that has long been familiar in the Inns of Court. Dickens, who knew all about them, thought that it was the gloom and isolation of the sets of the inns that had reduced them to their dismal apathy and misery. It may be so, or it is possible that the solemn air of antiquity and retirement in the heart of London appeals to men of retired and melancholy habit. I have been long absent from the courts and squares and buildings, and I do not know whether the silent men still resort in these places.

It was an accident that introduced me to one of them. One June night, about ten o'clock, when the sky was still luminous, I was strolling round the Square, and was just passing one of the brotherhood of the night, when he slipped on something on the pavement, and fell sideways, very awkwardly. I helped him up at once, and put him on his feet, and he gave a cry of pain as I did so. He had sprained or strained his ankle muscle, and was evidently in anguish when he tried to set the foot on the ground. I told him to lean on me, and I would see him home. He said his name was Mansel, and he gave me his number; one of the top sets on the west side of the Square. I got him up the stairs with a good deal of difficulty, took his key and supported him to his arm-chair by the fire-place. Then I suggested fetching the doctor from Warwick Place; but he wouldn't hear of that. 'We will see how it feels after a good night's rest. I don't like sending for the doctor; you never know what they may say.'

I expressed my doubts as to the effects of the night's rest, and proposed that I should leave him in his candle-lit room.

'I wish you would sit down and keep me company for an hour, if you can spare the time. Light your pipe—I've seen you smoking in the square—and if you don't mind going to that cupboard, I think you'll find some whiskey there, and glasses, and a jug of water.'

The whiskey bottle was unopened and dusty, and I searched at his direction in a drawer for the corkscrew. I set a glass beside him, and was about to pour, when he checked me with a gesture, and a 'help yourself.' And then, relenting, he said: 'I think I will have a little tonight. I am still feeling rather shaky.' But he stopped me when about a tablespoonful had gone into the glass, and added water largely, and so made himself a ghostly and ineffectual drink.

The Exalted Omega

We began to talk. He told me he had been living in the inn for four or five years; he didn't seem certain as to the precise duration of his residence.

'One gets a little vague, don't you think, living in these old rooms, looking down on the trees,' he apologised, 'and, somehow, I have rather fallen out of the way of seeing people, and getting about, and so forth, and so forth. One drifts along from day to day, rather sluggishly and ineffectually, I'm afraid . . . and, the edges get dulled, I suppose.'

He was a man in the early or middle thirties by his looks: a slight, dark man, with small features, and nothing very distinctive or distinguished about him.

He was difficult to talk to. He never read the papers, he told me. He spoke with a glint of fervour about his old home in the west, of waterbrooks in still hidden valleys, of the wild outlands where no one came, of the sun shining on the bracken on the mountain-side, of the grove of ash trees and their magic.

'*Hic vox sine clamore sonat; hic saltat et cantat chorus nympharum eternus.*' He spoke as if he were quoting some familiar text.

He drifted on, in his own terms, rather sluggishly and ineffectually. I noted that book-cases, well filled, took up a great part of the wall space.

'You have at least good company there,' I said, pointing to the shelves.

'Well, I have read a good deal in my time. Yes; I used to be a considerable reader—of a very unsystematic kind,

I may say. I never read a book that I didn't want to read. Nobody shall shove books down my throat. . . . But I find myself losing the habit of reading; I can't get the relish that I used to find in it. What did I say just now? The edges are dulled. . . . When a man finds *Tristram Shandy* flat, you know? I remember when I first read it, and for long after that, it was pure sorcery to me; a spell, a spell.'

He took up the book from the little table by his chair, and handed it to me as if in illustration of what he had just said. It was an early nineteenth century edition, rather shabbily printed.

I turned over the leaves of the great fantasy, and something on the fly-leaf caught my attention: an odd mark or symbol; the mark that I have described as an omega on a stick. We talked a little longer, and then I left him, with the hope that he might find the remedy of a night's rest efficient in the cure of the twisted ankle. He looked a disconsolate figure in his chair in the dim room, with the misty night in the plane trees of the inn garden as a background.

The next day my business took me up north, among the singing voices of Northumberland. I was away for nearly a week, and when I got back there were evening engagements and amusements to occupy me. I must have been ten days before leisure and a pale green sky led me to take my stroll about the Square. Three or four of the usual nocturnal company were dawdling and creeping round the pavement in the usual manner; but there was no sign of Mansel. I knew it would be of no use to ask about him from these men; it was not likely that any one of them would know his name. I went up his stair, and knocked at the black door. There was no reply, no sound. I waited and knocked again and louder: still, nothing. For a third time I beat my summons, and then there were slow footsteps sounding along the passage. The door was opened; and there stood Mansel, carrying a candle; and the light of it showed a face of strong distaste for the caller; for any caller. But he relaxed a little when he saw me, and asked me to follow him. He was still limping from the injury of ten days before. No doubt, he had tried neither care nor cure.

'It hasn't troubled me much,' he remarked when we sat down. 'If I had wanted to get about it would have been tiresome, I daresay. But then, I never do want to get about. I hardly ever go beyond the inn gates. I have seen it all, I don't want to see it again.'

He spoke a little of his reading, which had become, he repeated, distasteful to him.

'You get to the end of it all,' he murmured. 'Or, so I have found. Everywhere, you come to a blank wall. Every path and track you take ends with a blank wall. Not read everything? No indeed; I have neglected vast deserts of dullness. Would you advise me to try Mommsen, or Professor Freeman, or Darwin? Science deals with surfaces; what have I to do with surfaces?'

—I was saying that Dickens knew about the solitaries of the Inns of Court. As Mansel was talking his weary nonsense, about coming to the end of everything, of being brought up by a blank wall whatever track he took, I was reminded very strongly of Mr Parkle's friend in 'Chambers'.

One dry hot autumn evening at twilight, this man, being then turned of fifty, looked in upon Parkle in his usual lounging way, with his cigar in his mouth as usual, and said: 'I am going out of town.' As he never went out of town Parkle said: 'Oh, indeed! At last?' 'Yes,' says he, 'at last. For what is a man to do? London is so small! If you go west, you come to Hounslow. If you go east, you come to Bow. If you go south, there's Brixton or Norwood. If you go north, you can't get rid of Barnet.

It struck me as odd that two such different people as the actual Mansel and the Dickens' character should reach the same end by their varying ways. The blank wall loomed equally before them. I hoped that Mansel would not find at last the same end as Parkle's friend; the end of a suicide's rope.

I tried to stir the man a little out of his apathy. I misquoted a well-known passage of a well-known writer; and he flickered into a faint gleam of interest.

'Not quite that, is it? "We are all as God made us, and many of us a great deal worse." Surely. "and often a great deal worse"? Would you mind verifying? There's the book, at the end of the second shelf.'

'I verified the *Don Quixote* quotation; and he nodded a very brief satisfaction at having the phrase correctly. I was putting the book back in its place, and it slipped from my hand to the floor. As I picked it up, I noticed again the mark of the omega; this time on the title page.

'May I ask,' I said, 'if this odd omega in your books has any particular meaning?'

He smiled faintly. 'That,' he explained, 'is a bit of schoolboy nonsense. I don't recollect whether it was because I was proud of having learnt the Greek alphabet; but I got into the way of putting that thing in my books instead of my name or initials, and I kept it up afterwards. You would find it in every book on the shelves, and sometimes I've used it to mark a passage, in the margin. Indeed, I used to sign my letters to old friends with the Omega Exalted, as I called it.'

I stayed on at Gray's Inn for the next six or seven months, and I suppose I repeated my visit to Mansel three or four times. I could not say that I was welcome, but I was not exactly unwelcome. It was a pang for him to open his door, but he was not displeased to let me in. There was no change in him, no sign that he would revive, and live again like other men. Then I left London, and remained away for many years, and I cannot say that Mansel was much more than a dim image in my memory. On my return, finding myself one day in Holborn, it struck me that I might make some enquiries. They told me in the inn that Mr Mansel was understood to be very infirm; that he had not been seen outside his chambers for years and years. I thought I had better not look him up; he would not remember me or desire to do so.

A year ago his laundress found him dead in his chair next to the fire-place. It appeared on examination that his heart had given out. He had left his money and his goods to a distant cousin in the west, who came up to town, did what was necessary, and went down again to some obscure retreat by the sunset. Mansel's books and furniture—there was nothing of value—were sold and dispersed.

The inn painted and papered the set of rooms on the top floor of the Square, and made them look as gay as they could look. But they did not let readily. There were plenty of applicants, but I gathered that people who came in a hurry to secure chambers giving on the garden, drew back when they were taken into the set. Something seemed amiss; they could not say what. They didn't 'fancy' the place. Everything in the way of decoration, it was allowed, was extremely bright and cheerful. One prospective tenant, it was a lady, was seized with a fit of shivering and said she felt as if icy water were trickling down her spine. It must have been nine or ten months after Mansel's death that the set was taken by a young couple, who seemed to think themselves lucky, and made no complaint as to 'something' or anything. The gentleman was connected with finance, and the lady was gaiety itself. She had a loud and cheerful voice, and a louder laugh, and expressed herself, so it was said, with consid-

erable freedom. These people laid themselves out to
brighten things. They gave frequent parties, a little on the
loud side, it was thought, for the Inn, and the porters at
the Holborn Gate were busy long after midnight.

And then, all this liveliness came to an end in a very
tragic manner. In the middle of a 'bottle party', when
everything was at a high pitch, one of the guests, a Mr
Jerome Platt, understood to be a cousin of the host's,
suddenly complained of agonising internal pains. He was
taken to the hotel where he was staying, and doctors were
summoned, and everything done that could be done. But
Mr Platt died the next day; of acute ptomaine poisoning
as the evidence at the inquest demonstrated. He had
dined at a fashionable West End restaurant before going
on to the party at Gray's Inn. There were no complaints
from any other of the diners.

By the end of the month, old Mansel's rooms were
again vacant. The bright tenants, very naturally, as people
said, felt they could not go on living in a place where such
a terrible thing had happened. They were supposed to
have gone abroad within three weeks of the disastrous
'bottle party'.

And as to that very different party given by Mrs
Ladislaw, and the end of it, and the scribble on the paper?
So far as I can make out from what Welling has told me,
the Ladislaw séance must have taken place a day, or
perhaps two days, before that grim gathering in Gray's
Inn. Mansel had been dead for many months: what are

we to infer? Had he anything to do with the seizure of the medium, and with what was written by her?

There is one point that should not be forgotten. I noted that, in Welling's opinion, the corrupt Latin 'messages' written by Miss Tuke might very well be subconscious memories, imperfectly preserved, of something she had read without understanding years before, and which had entirely disappeared from her conscious mind. So, perhaps, with the 'exalted omega'. Mansel's books had been dispersed. None of them was of any interest to the big second-hand booksellers, to the dealers in rarities; the volumes would therefore tend to find their way to the small shops and the poorer neighbourhoods. Mrs Ladislaw might very well have passed such shops on her marketing rounds; she might have turned over the books in the threepenny and sixpenny boxes—and she might easily have seen old Mansel's omega mark; very likely without consciously noting it.

It is distinctly possible that this is the solution of the problem; though here also there are lurking difficulties and obscurities.

The Children of the Pool

A COUPLE of summers ago I was staying with old friends in my native county, on the Welsh border. It was in the heat and drought of a hot and dry year, and I came into those green, well-watered valleys with a sense of a great refreshment. Here was relief from the burning of London streets, from the close and airless nights, when all the myriad walls of brick and stone and concrete and the pavements that are endless give out into the heavy darkness the fires that all day long have been drawn from the sun. And from those roadways that have become like railways, with their changing lamps, and their yellow globes, and their bars and studs of steel; from the menace of instant death if your feet stray from the track: from all this what a rest to walk under the green leaf in quiet, and hear the stream trickling from the heart of the hill.

My friends were old friends, and they were urgent that I should go my own way. There was breakfast at nine, but it was equally serviceable and excellent at ten; and I could be in for something cold for lunch, if I liked; and if I didn't like I could stay away till dinner at half-past seven; and then there was all the evening for talks about old times and about the changes, with comfortable drinks, and bed soothed by memories and tobacco, and by the brook that twisted under dark alders through the meadow below. And not a red bungalow to be seen for many a mile around! Sometimes, when the heat even in that green land was more than burning, and the wind from the mountains in the west ceased, I would stay all day under shade on the lawn, but more often I went a-field and trod remembered ways, and tried to find new ones, in that happy and bewildered country. There, paths go wandering into undiscovered valleys, there from deep and narrow lanes with overshadowing hedges, still smaller tracks that I suppose are old bridle-paths, creep obscurely, obviously leading nowhere in particular.

It was on a day of cooler air that I went adventuring abroad on such an expedition. It was a 'day of the veil'. There were no clouds in the sky, but a high mist, grey and luminous, had been drawn all over it. At one moment, it would seem that the sun must shine through, and the blue appear; and then the trees in the wood would seem to blossom, and the meadows lightened; and then again the veil would be drawn. I struck off by the stony lane that led from the back of the house up over the hill; I had last gone that way a-many years ago, of a winter afternoon, when the ruts were frozen into hard ridges, and dark pines on high places rose above snow, and the sun was red and still above the mountain. I remembered that the way had given good sport, with twists to right and left, and unexpected descents, and then risings to places of

thorn and bracken, till it darkened to the hushed stillness
of a winter's night, and I turned homeward reluctant.
Now I took another chance with all the summer day
before me, and resolved to come to some end and
conclusion of the matter.

I think I had gone beyond the point at which I had
stopped and turned back as the frozen darkness and the
bright stars came on me. I remembered the dip in the
hedge, from which I saw the round tumulus on high at
the end of the mountain wall; and there was the white
farm on the hillside, and the farmer was still calling to his
dog, as he—or his father—had called before, his voice
high and thin in the distance. After this point, I seemed to
be in undiscovered country; the ash trees grew densely on
either side of the way and met above it: I went on and on
into the unknown in the manner of the only good guide-
books, which are the tales of old knights.

The road went down, and climbed, and again de-
scended, all through the deep of the wood. Then, on both
sides, the trees ceased, though the hedges were so high
that I could see nothing of the way of the land about me.
And just at the wood's ending, there was one of those
tracks or little paths of which I have spoken, going off
from my lane on the right, and winding out of sight
quickly under all its leafage of hazel and wild rose, maple
and hornbeam, with a holly here and there, and honey-
suckle golden, and dark briony shining and twining
everywhere. I could not resist the invitation of a path so
obscure and uncertain, and set out on its track of green

and profuse grass, with the ground beneath still soft to the feet, even in the drought of that fiery summer. The way wound, as far as I could make out, on the slope of a hill, neither ascending nor descending, and after a mile or more of this rich walking, it suddenly ceased, and I found myself on a bare hillside, on a rough track that went down to a grey house. It was now a farm by its looks and surroundings, but there were signs of old state about it: good sixteenth-century mullioned windows and a Jacobean porch projecting from the centre, with dim armorial bearings mouldering above the door.

It struck me that bread and cheese and cider would be grateful, and I beat upon the door with my stick, and brought a pleasant woman to open it.

'Do you think,' I began, 'you could be so good as . . .'

And then came a shout from somewhere at the end of the stone passage, and a great voice called:

'Come in, then, come in, you old scoundrel, if your name is Meyrick, as I'm sure it is.'

I was amazed. The pleasant woman grinned and said:

'It seems you are well known here, sir, already. But perhaps you had heard that Mr Roberts was staying here.'

My old acquaintance, James Roberts, came tumbling out from his den at the back. He was a man whom I had known a long time, but not very well. Our affairs in London moved on different lines, and so we did not often meet. But I was glad to see him in that unexpected place: he was a round man, always florid and growing redder in the face with his years. He was a countryman of mine, but

I had hardly known him before we both went to town, since his home had been at the northern end of the county.

He shook me cordially by the hand, and looked as if he would like to smack me on the back—he was, a little, that kind of man—and repeated his 'Come in, come in!' adding to the pleasant woman: 'And bring you another plate, Mrs Morgan, and all the rest of it. I hope you've not forgotten how to eat Caerphilly cheese, Meyrick. I can tell you, there is none better than Mrs Morgan's making. And, Mrs Morgan, another jug of cider, and *seidr dda*, mind you.'

I never knew whether he had been brought up as a boy to speak Welsh. In London, he had lost all but the faintest trace of accent, but down here in Gwent, the tones of the country had richly returned to him; and he smacked as strongly of the land in his speech as the cheerful farmer's wife herself. I judged his accent was a part of his holiday.

He drew me into the little parlour with its old furniture and its pleasant old-fashioned ornaments and faintly flowering wallpaper, and set me in an elbow-chair at the round table, and gave me, as I told him, exactly what I had meant to ask for; bread and cheese and cider. All very good; Mrs Morgan, it was clear, had the art of making a Caerphilly cheese that was succulent—a sort of white *bel paese*—far different from those dry and stony cheeses that often bring dishonour on the Caerphilly name. And afterwards there was gooseberry jam and cream. And the tobacco that the country uses: 'Shag-on-the-Back', from the Welsh Back, Bristol. And then there was gin.

This last we partook of out-of-doors, in an old stone summer-house, in the garden at the side. A white rose had grown all over the summer-house, and shaded and glorified it. The water in the big jug had just been drawn from the well in the limestone rock—and I told Roberts gratefully that I felt a great deal better than when I had knocked at the farmhouse door. I told him where I was staying—he knew my host by name—and he, in turn, informed me that it was his first visit to Lanypwll, as the farm was called. A neighbour of his at Lee had recommended Mrs Morgan's cooking very highly: and, as he said, you couldn't speak too well of her in that way or any other.

We sipped and smoked through the afternoon in that pleasant retreat under the white roses. I meditated gratefully on the fact that I should not dare to enjoy 'Shag-on-the-Back' so freely in London: a potent tobacco, of full and ripe savour, but not for the hard streets.

'You say the farm is called Lanypwll,' I interjected, 'that means "by the pool", doesn't it? Where is the pool? I don't see it.'

'Come you,' said Roberts, 'and I will show you.'

He took me by a little gate through the garden hedge of laurels, thick and high, and round to the left of the house, the opposite side to that by which I had made my approach. And there we climbed a green rounded bastion of the old ages, and he pointed down to a narrow valley, shut in by steep wooded hills. There at the bottom was a level, half-marshland and half-black water lying in still pools, with green islands of iris and of all manner of rank and strange growths that love to have their roots in slime.

'There is your pool for you,' said Roberts.

It was the most strange place, I thought, hidden away under the hills as if it were a secret. The steeps that went down to it were a tangle of undergrowth, of all manner of boughs mingled, with taller trees rising above the mass, and down at the edge of the marsh some of these had perished in the swampy water, and stood white and bare and ghastly, with leprous limbs.

'An ugly looking place,' I said to Roberts.

'I quite agree with you. It is an ugly place enough. They tell me at the farm it's not safe to go near it, or you may get fever and I don't know what else. And, indeed, if you didn't go down carefully and watch your steps, you might easily find yourself up to the neck in that black muck there.'

We turned back into the garden and to our summer-house, and soon after, it was time for me to make my way home.

'How long are you staying with Nichol?' Roberts asked me, as we parted. I told him, and he insisted on my dining with him at the end of the week.

'I will "send" you,' he said. 'I will take you by a short cut across the fields and see that you don't lose your way. Roast duck and green peas,' he added alluringly, 'and something good for the digestion afterwards.'

The Children of the Pool

It was a fine evening when I next journeyed to the farm, but indeed we got tired of saying 'fine weather' throughout that wonderful summer. I found Roberts cheery and welcoming, but, I thought, hardly in such rosy spirits as on my former visit. We were having a cocktail of his composition in the summer-house, as the famous duck gained the last glow of brown perfection; and I noticed that his speech was not bubbling so freely from him as before. He fell silent once or twice and looked thoughtful. He told me he'd ventured down to the pool, the swampy place at the bottom. 'And it looks no better when you see it close at hand. Black, oily stuff that isn't like water, with a scum upon it, and weeds like a lot of monsters. I never saw such queer, ugly plants. There's one rank-looking thing down there covered with dull crimson blossoms, all bloated out and speckled like a toad.'

'You're no botanist,' I remarked.

'No, not I. I know buttercups and daisies and not much more. Mrs Morgan here was quite frightened when I told her where I'd been. She said she hoped I mightn't be sorry for it. But I feel as well as ever. I don't think there are many places left in the country now where you can get malaria.'

We proceeded to the duck and the green peas and rejoiced in their perfection. There was some very old ale that Mr Morgan had bought when an ancient tavern in the neighbourhood had been pulled down; its age and original excellence had combined to make a drink like a rare wine. The 'something good for the digestion' turned out to be a mellow brandy that Roberts had brought with him from town. I told him that I had never known a better hour. He warmed up with the good meat and drink and was cheery enough; and yet I thought there was a reserve, something obscure at the back of his mind that was by no means cheerful.

We had a second glass of the mellow brandy, and Roberts, after a moment's indecision, spoke out. He dropped his holiday game of Welsh countryman completely.

'You wouldn't think, would you,' he began, 'that a man would come down to a place like this to be blackmailed at the end of the journey?'

'Good Lord!' I gasped in amazement, 'I should think not indeed. What's happened?'

He looked very grave. I thought even that he looked frightened.

'Well, I'll tell you. A couple of nights ago, I went for a stroll after my dinner; a beautiful night, with the moon shining, and a nice, clean breeze. So I walked up over the hill, and then took the path that leads down through the wood to the brook. I'd got into the wood, fifty yards or so, when I heard my name called out: "Roberts! James Roberts!" in a shrill, piercing voice, a young girl's voice, and I jumped pretty well out of my skin, I can tell you. I stopped dead and stared all about me, Of course I could see nothing at all—bright moonlight and black shadow and all those trees—anybody could hide. Then it came to me that it was some girl of the place having a game with her sweetheart: James Roberts is a common enough name, especially in this part of the country. So I was just going on, not bothering my head about the local love-affairs, when that scream came right in my ear: "Roberts! Roberts! James Roberts!"—and then half-a-dozen words that I won't trouble you with; not yet, at any rate.'

I have said that Roberts was by no means an intimate friend of mine. But I had always known him as a genial, cordial fellow, a thoroughly good-natured man; and I was sorry and shocked, too, to see him sitting there wretched and dismayed. He looked as if he had seen a ghost; he looked much worse than that. He looked as if he had seen Terror.

But it was too early to press him closely. I said:

'What did you do then?'

'I turned about, and ran back through the wood, and tumbled over the stile. I got home here as quick as ever I could, and shut myself up in this room; dripping with fright and gasping for breath. I was almost crazy, I believe. I walked up and down. I sat down in the chair and got up again. I wondered whether I should wake up in my bed and find I'd been having a nightmare. I cried at last. I'll tell you the truth: I put my head in my hands, and the tears ran down my cheeks. I was quite broken.'

'But, look here,' I said, 'isn't this making a great to-do about very little? I can quite see it must have been a nasty shock. But, how long did you say you had been staying here; ten days, was it?'

'A fortnight, tomorrow.'

'Well; you know country ways as well as I do. You may
be sure that everybody within three or four miles of
Lanypwll knows about a gentleman from London, a Mr
James Roberts, staying at the farm. And there are always
unpleasant young people to be found, wherever you go. I
gather that this girl used very abusive language when she
hailed you. She probably thought it was a good joke. You
had taken that walk through the wood in the evening a
couple of times before? No doubt, you had been noticed
going that way, and the girl and her friend or friends
planned to give you a shock. I wouldn't think any more of
it, if I were you.'

He almost cried out.

'Think any more of it! What will the world think of it?'

There was an anguish of terror in his voice. I thought it
was time to come to cues. I spoke up pretty briskly:

'Now, look here, Roberts, it's no good beating about
the bush. Before we can do anything, we've got to have
the whole tale, fair and square. What I've gathered is this:
you go for a walk in a wood near here one evening, and a
girl—you say it was a girl's voice—hails you by your
name, and then screams out a lot of filthy language. Is
there anything more in it than that?'

'There's a lot more than that. I was going to ask you
not to let it go any further; but as far as I can see, there
won't be any secret in it much longer. There's another
end to the story, and it goes back a good many years—to

the time when I first came to London as a young man. That's twenty-five years ago.'

He stopped speaking. When he began again, I could feel that he spoke with unutterable repugnance. Every word was a horror to him.

'You know as well as I do, that there are all sorts of turnings in London that a young fellow can take; good, bad, and indifferent. There was a good deal of bad luck about it. I do believe, and I was too young to know or care much where I was going; but I got into a turning with the black pit at the end of it.'

He beckoned me to lean forward across the table, and whispered for a minute or two in my ear. In my turn, I heard not without horror. I said nothing.

'*That* was what I heard shrieked out in the wood. What do you say?'

'You've done with all that long ago?'

'It was done with very soon after it was begun. It was no more than a bad dream. And then it all flashed back on me like deadly lightning. What do you say? What can I do?'

I told him that I had to admit that it was no good to try to put the business in the wood down to accident, the casual filthy language of a depraved village girl. As I said, it couldn't be a case of a bow drawn at a venture.

'There must be somebody behind it. Can you think of anybody?'

'There may be one or two left. I can't say. I haven't heard of any of them for years. I thought they had all gone; dead, or at the other side of the world.'

'Yes; but people can get back from the other side of the world pretty quickly in these days. Yokohama is not much farther off than Yarmouth. But you haven't heard of any of these people lately?'

'As I said; not for years. But the secret's out.'

'But, let's consider. Who is this girl? Where does she live? We must get at her, and try if we can't frighten the life out of her. And, in the first place, we'll find out the source of her information. Then we shall know where we are. I suppose you have discovered who she is?'

'I've not a notion of who she is or where she lives.'

'I daresay you wouldn't care to ask the Morgans any questions. But to go back to the beginning: you spoke of blackmail. Did this damned girl ask you for money to shut her mouth?'

'No; I shouldn't have called it blackmail. She didn't say anything about money.'

'Well; that sounds more hopeful. Let's see; tonight is Saturday. You took this unfortunate walk of yours a couple of nights ago; on Thursday night. And you haven't heard anything more since. I should keep away from that wood, and try to find out who the young lady is. That's the first thing to be done, clearly.'

I was trying to cheer him up a little; but he only stared at me with his horror-stricken eyes.

'It didn't finish with the wood,' he groaned. 'My bedroom is next door to this room where we are. When I had pulled myself together a bit that night, I had a stiff glass, about double my allowance, and went off to bed and to sleep. I woke up with a noise of tapping at the window, just by the head of the bed. Tap, tap, tap, it went. I thought it might be a bough beating on the glass. And then I heard that voice calling me: "James Roberts: open, open!"

'I tell you, my flesh crawled on my bones. I would have cried out, but I couldn't make a sound. The moon had gone down, and there's a great old pear tree close to the window, and it was quite dark. I sat up in my bed, shaking for fear. It was dead still, and I began to think that the fright I had got in the wood had given me a nightmare. Then the voice called again, and louder:

' "James Roberts! Open. Quick."

'And I had to open. I leaned half out of bed, and got at the latch, and opened the window a little. I didn't dare to look out. But it was too dark to see anything in the shadow of the tree. And then she began to talk to me. She told me all about it from the beginning. She knew all the names. She knew where my business was in London, and where I lived, and who my friends were. She said that they should all know. And she said: "And you yourself shall tell them, and you shall not be able to keep back a single word!" '

The wretched man fell back in his chair, shuddering and gasping for breath. He beat his hands up and down, with a gesture of hopeless fear and misery; and his lips grinned with dread.

I won't say that I began to see light. But I saw a hint of certain possibilities of light or—let us say—of a lessening of the darkness. I said a soothing word or two, and let him get a little more quiet. The telling of this extraordinary and very dreadful experience had set his nerves all dancing; and yet, having made a clean breast of it all, I could see that he felt some relief. His hands lay quiet on the table, and his lips ceased their horrible grimacing. He looked at me with a faint expectancy, I thought; as if he had begun to cherish a dim hope that I might have some sort of help for him. He could not see himself the possibility of rescue; still, one never knew what resources and freedoms the other man might bring.

That, at least, was what his poor, miserable face seemed to me to express; and I hoped I was right, and let him simmer a little, and gather to himself such twigs and straws of hope as he could. Then, I began again:

'This was on the Thursday night. And last night? Another visit?'

'The same as before. Almost word for word.'

'And it was all true, what she said? The girl was not lying?'

'Every word of it was true. There were some things that I had forgotten myself; but when she spoke of them, I remembered at once. There was the number of a house in a certain street, for example. If you had asked me for that number a week ago I should have told you, quite honestly, that I knew nothing about it. But when I heard it, I knew it in the instant: I could see that number in the light of a street lamp. The sky was dark and cloudy, and a bitter wind was blowing, and driving the leaves on the pavement—that November night.'

'When the fire was lit?'

'That night. When they appeared.'

'And you haven't seen this girl? You couldn't describe her?'

'I was afraid to look; I told you. I waited when she stopped speaking. I sat there for half an hour or an hour. Then I lit my candle and shut the window-latch. It was three o'clock and growing light.'

I was thinking it over. I noted that Roberts confessed that every word spoken by his visitant was true. She had sprung no surprises on him; there had been no suggestion of fresh details, names, or circumstances. That struck me as having a certain—possible—significance; and the knowledge of Roberts's present circumstances, his City address, and his home address, and the names of his friends: that was interesting, too.

There was a glimpse of a possible hypothesis. I could not be sure; but I told Roberts that I thought something might be done. To begin with, I said, I was going to keep him company for the night. Nichol would guess that I had shirked the walk home after nightfall; that would be quite all right. And in the morning he was to pay Mrs Morgan for the two extra weeks he had arranged to stay, with something by way of compensation. 'And it should be something handsome,' I added with emotion, thinking of the duck and the old ale. 'And then,' I finished, 'I shall pack you off to the other side of the island.'

Of that old ale I made him drink a liberal dose by way of sleeping-draught. He hardly needed a hypnotic; the terror that he had endured and the stress of telling it had worn him out. I saw him fall into bed and fall asleep in a moment, and I curled up, comfortably enough, in a roomy armchair. There was no trouble in the night, and when I writhed myself awake, I saw Roberts sleeping peacefully. I let him alone, and wandered about the house and the shining morning garden, till I came upon Mrs Morgan, busy in the kitchen.

I broke the trouble to her. I told her that I was afraid that the place was not agreeing at all with Mr Roberts. 'Indeed,' I said, 'he was taken so ill last night that I was afraid to leave him. His nerves seem to be in a very bad way.'

'Indeed, then, I don't wonder at all,' replied Mrs Morgan, with a very grave face. But I wondered a good deal at this remark of hers, not having a notion as to what she meant.

I went on to explain what I had arranged for our patient, as I called him: East Coast breezes, and crowds of people, the noisier the better, and, indeed, that was the cure that I had in mind. I said that I was sure Mr Roberts would do the proper thing.

'That will be all right, sir, I am sure: don't you trouble yourself about that. But the sooner you get him away after I have given you both your breakfasts, the better I shall be pleased. I am frightened to death for him, I can tell you.'

And she went off to her work, murmuring something that sounded like 'Plant y pwll, plant y pwll'.

I gave Roberts no time for reflection. I woke him up, bustled him out of bed, hurried him through his breakfast, saw him pack his suitcase, make his farewells to the Morgans, and had him sitting in the shade on Nichol's lawn well before the family were back from church. I gave Nichol a vague outline of the circumstances—nervous breakdown and so forth—introduced them to one another, and left them talking about the Black Mountains, Roberts's land of origin. The next day I saw him off at the station, on his way to Great Yarmouth, via London. I told him with an air of authority that he would have no more trouble, 'from any quarter,' I emphasised. And he was to write to me at my town address in a week's time.

'And, by the way,' I said, just before the train slid along the platform, 'here's a bit of Welsh for you. What does "plant y pwll" mean? Something of the pool?'

' "Plant y pwll," ' he explained, 'means "children of the pool." '

When my holiday was ended, and I had got back to town, I began my investigations into the case of James Roberts and his nocturnal visitant. When he began his story I was extremely distressed—I made no doubt as to the bare truth of it, and was shocked to think of a very kindly man threatened with overwhelming disgrace and disaster. There seemed nothing impossible in the tale stated at large, and in the first outline. It is not altogether unheard of for very decent men to have had a black patch in their lives, which they have done their best to live down and atone for and forget. Often enough, the explanation of such misadventure is not hard to seek. You have a young fellow, very decently but very simply brought up among simple country people, suddenly pitched into the labyrinth of London, into a maze in which there are many turnings, as the unfortunate Roberts put it, which lead to disaster, or to something blacker than disaster. The more experienced man, the man of keen instincts and perceptions, knows the aspect of these tempting passages and avoids them; some have the wit to turn back in time; a few are caught in the trap at the end. And in some cases, though there may be apparent escape, and peace and security for many years, the teeth of the snare are about the man's leg all the while, and close at last on highly reputable chairmen and churchwardens and pillars of all sorts of seemly institutions. And then gaol, or at best, hissing and extinction.

So, on the first face of it, I was by no means prepared to pooh-pooh Roberts's tale. But when he came to detail, and I had time to think it over, that entirely illogical faculty, which sometimes takes charge of our thoughts and judgements, told me that there was some huge flaw in all this, that somehow or other, things had not happened so. This mental process, I may say, is strictly indefinable and unjustifiable by any laws of thought that I have ever heard of. It won't do to take our stand with Bishop Butler, and declare with him that probability is the guide of life; deducing from this premise the conclusion that the improbable doesn't happen. Any man who cares to glance over his experience of the world and of things in general is aware that the most wildly improbable events are constantly happening. For example, I take up today's paper, sure that I shall find something to my purpose, and in a minute I come across the headline: 'Damaging a Model Elephant'. A father, evidently a man of substance, accuses his son of this strange offence. Last summer, the father told the court, his son constructed in their front garden a large model of an elephant, the material being bought by witness. The skeleton of the elephant was made of tubing, and it was covered with soil and fibre, and held together with wire-netting. Flowers were planted on it, and it cost £3 5s.

A photograph of the elephant was produced in court, and the clerk remarked: 'It is a fearsome-looking thing.'

And then the catastrophe. The son got to know a married woman much older than himself, and his parents frowned, and there were quarrels. And so, one night, the young man came to his father's house, jumped over the garden wall and tried to push the elephant over. Failing, he proceeded to disembowel the elephant with a pair of wire clippers.

There! Nothing can be much more improbable than that tale, but it all happened so, as the *Daily Telegraph* assures me, and I believe every word of it. And I have no doubt that if I care to look I shall find something as improbable, or even more improbable, in the newspaper columns three or perhaps four times a week. What about the old man, unknown, unidentified, found in the Thames: in one pocket, a stone Buddha; in the other, a leather wallet, with the inscription: 'The hen that sits on the china egg is best off'?

The improbable happens and is constantly happening; but, using that faculty which I am unable to define, I rejected Roberts's girl of the wood and the window. I did not suspect him for a moment of leg-pulling of an offensive and vicious kind. His misery and terror were too clearly manifest for that, and I was certain that he was suffering from a very serious and dreadful shock—and yet I didn't believe in the truth of the story he had told me. I felt convinced that there was no girl in the case; either in the wood or at the window. And when Roberts told me, with increased horror, that every word she spoke was true, that she had even reminded him of matters that he had himself forgotten, I was greatly encouraged in my growing surmise. For, it seemed to me at least probable that if the case had been such as he supposed it, there would have been new and damning circumstances in the story, utterly unknown to him and unsuspected by him. But, as it was, everything that he was told he accepted; as a man in a dream accepts without hesitation the wildest fantasies as matters and incidents of his daily experience. Decidedly, there was no girl there.

The Children of the Pool

On the Sunday that he spent with me at the Wern, Nichol's place, I took advantage of his calmer condition—the night's rest had done him good—to get some facts and dates out of him, and when I returned to town, I put these to the test. It was not altogether an easy investigation since, on the surface, at least, the matters to be investigated were eminently trivial; the early days of a young man from the country up in London in a business house; and twenty-five years ago. Even really exciting murder trials and changes of ministries become blurred and uncertain in outline, if not forgotten, in twenty-five years, or in twelve years for that matter: and compared with such events, the affair of James Roberts seemed perilously like nothing at all.

However, I made the best use I could of the information that Roberts had given me; and I was fortified for the task by a letter I received from him. He told me that there had been no recurrence of the trouble (as he expressed it), that he felt quite well, and was enjoying himself immensely at Yarmouth. He said that the shows and entertainments on the sands were doing him 'no end of good. There's a Retired Executioner who does his old business in a tent, with the drop and everything, And there's a bloke who calls himself Archbishop of London, who fasts in a glass case, with his mitre and all his togs on.' Certainly, my patient was either recovered, or in a very fair way to recovery: I could set about my researches in a calm spirit of scientific curiosity, without the nervous tension of the surgeon called upon at short notice to perform a life-or-death operation.

As a matter of fact it was all more simple than I thought it would be. True, the results were nothing, or almost nothing, but that was exactly what I had expected and hoped. With the slight sketch of his early career in London, furnished me by Roberts, the horrors omitted by my request; with a name or two and a date or two, I got along very well. And what did it come to? Simply this: here was a lad—he was just seventeen—who had been brought up amongst lonely hills and educated at a small grammar school, furnished through a London uncle with a very small stool in a City office. By arrangement, settled after a long and elaborate correspondence, he was to board with some distant cousins, who lived in the Cricklewood-Kilburn-Brondesbury region, and with them he settled down, comfortably enough, as it seemed, though Cousin Ellen objected to his learning to smoke in his bedroom, and begged him to desist. The household consisted of Cousin Ellen, her husband, Henry Watts, and the two daughters, Helen and Justine. Justine was about Roberts's own age; Helen three or four years older. Mr Watts had married rather late in life, and had retired from his office a year or so before. He interested himself chiefly in tuberous-rooted begonias, and in the season went out a few miles to his cricket club and watched the game on Saturday afternoons. Every morning there was breakfast at eight, every evening there was high tea at seven, and in the meantime young Roberts did his best in the City, and liked his job well enough. He was shy with the two girls at first, but Justine was lively, and couldn't help having a voice like a peacock, and Helen was adorable. And so things went on very pleasantly for a year or perhaps eighteen months; on this basis, that Justine was a great joke, and that Helen was adorable. The trouble was that Justine didn't think that she was a great joke.

For, it must be said that Roberts's stay with his cousins ended in disaster. I rather gather that the young man and the quiet Helen were guilty of—shall we say—amiable indiscretions, though without serious consequences. But it appeared that Cousin Justine, a girl with black eyes and black hair, made discoveries which she resented savagely, denouncing the offenders at the top of that piercing voice of hers, in the waste hours of the Brondesbury night, to the immense rage, horror and consternation of the whole house. In fact, there was the devil to pay, and Mr Watts then and there turned young Roberts out of the house. And there is no doubt that he should have been thoroughly ashamed of himself. But young men. . . .

Nothing very much happened. Old Watts had cried in his rage that he would let Roberts's chief in the City hear the whole story; but, on reflection, he held his tongue. Roberts roamed about London for the rest of the night, refreshing himself occasionally at coffee-stalls. When the shops opened, he had a wash and brush-up, and was prompt and bright at his office. At midday, in the underground smoking-room of the tea-shop, he conferred with a fellow-clerk over their dominoes, and arranged to share rooms with him out Norwood way. From that point onwards, the career of James Roberts had been eminently quiet, uneventful, successful.

Now, everybody, I suppose, is aware that in recent years the silly business of Divination by Dreams has ceased to be a joke and has become a very serious science. It is called Psychoanalysis; and is compounded, I would say, by mingling one grain of sense with a hundred of pure nonsense. From the simplest and most obvious dreams, the psychoanalyst deduces the most incongruous and extravagant results. A black savage tells him that he has dreamed of being chased by lions, or, maybe, by crocodiles; and the psycho man knows at once that the black is suffering from the Oedipus-complex. That is, he is madly in love with his own mother, and is, therefore, afraid of the vengeance of his father. Everybody knows, of course, that 'lion' and 'crocodile' are symbols of 'father'. And I understand that there are educated people who believe this stuff.

It is all nonsense, to be sure; and so much the greater nonsense inasmuch as the true interpretation of many dreams—not by any means of all dreams—moves, it may be said, in the opposite direction to the method of psychoanalysis. The psychoanalyst infers the monstrous and abnormal from a trifle; it is often safe to reverse the process. If a man dreams that he has committed a sin before which the sun hid his face, it is often safe to conjecture that, in sheer forgetfulness, he wore a red tie, or brown boots with evening dress. A slight dispute with the vicar may deliver him in sleep into the clutches of the Spanish Inquisition, and the torment of a fiery death. Failure to catch the post with a rather important letter will sometimes bring a great realm to ruin in the world of dreams. And here, I have no doubt, we have the explanation or part of the explanation of the Roberts affair. Without question, he had been a bad boy; there was something more than a trifle at the heart of his trouble. But his original offence, grave as we may think it, had in his hidden consciousness, swollen and exaggerated itself into a monstrous mythology of evil. Some time ago, a learned and curious investigator demonstrated how Coleridge had taken a bald sentence from an old chronicler, and had made it the nucleus of *The Ancient Mariner*. With a vast gesture of the spirit, he had unconsciously gathered from all the four seas of his vast reading all manner of creatures into his net: till the bare hint of the old book glowed into one of the great masterpieces of the world's poetry. Roberts had nothing in him of the poetic faculty, nothing of the shaping power of the imagination, no trace of the gift of expression, by which the artist delivers his soul of its burden. In him, as in many men, there was a great gulf fixed between the hidden and the open consciousness; so that which could not come out into the light grew and swelled secretly, hugely, horribly in the darkness. If Roberts had been a poet or a painter or a musician; we might have had a masterpiece. As he was neither: we had a monster. And I do not at all believe that his years had consciously been vexed by a deep sense of guilt. I gathered in the course of my researches that not long after the flight from Brondesbury, Roberts was made aware of unfortunate incidents in the Watts Saga—if we may use this honoured term—which convinced him that there were extenuating circumstances in his offence, and excuses for his wrong-doing. The actual fact had, no doubt, been forgotten or remembered very slightly, rarely, casually, without any sense of grave moment or culpability attached to it; while, all the while, a pageantry of horror was being secretly formed in the hidden places of the man's soul. And at last, after the years of growth and swelling in the darkness; the monster leapt into the light, and with such violence that to the victim it seemed an actual and objective entity.

And, in a sense, it had risen from the black waters of the pool. I was reading a few days ago, in a review of a grave book on psychology, the following very striking sentences:

The things which we distinguish as qualities or values are inherent in the real environment to make the configuration that they do make with our sensory response to them. There is such a thing as a 'sad' landscape, even when we who look at it are feeling jovial; and if we think it is 'sad' only because we attribute to it something derived from our own past associations with sadness, Professor Koffka gives us good reason to regard the view as superficial. That is not imputing human attributes to what are described as 'demand characters' in the environment, but giving proper recognition to the other end of a nexus, of which only one end is organised in our own mind.

Psychology is, I am sure, a difficult and subtle science, which, perhaps naturally, must be expressed in subtle and difficult language. But so far as I can gather the sense of the passage which I have quoted, it comes to this: that a landscape, a certain configuration of wood, water, height and depth, light and dark, flower and rock, is, in fact, an objective reality, a thing; just as opium and wine are things, not clotted fancies, mere creatures of our make-believe, to which we give a kind of spurious reality and efficacy. The dreams of De Quincey were a synthesis of De Quincey, *plus* opium; the riotous gaiety of Charles Surface and his friends was the product and result of the wine they had drunk, *plus* their personalities. So, the profound Professor Koffka—his book is called *Principles of Gestalt Psychology*—insists that the 'sadness' which we attribute to a particular landscape is really and efficiently in the landscape and not merely in ourselves; and consequently that the landscape can affect us and produce results in us, in precisely the same manner as drugs and meat and drink affect us in their several ways. Poe, who knew many secrets, knew this, and taught that landscape gardening was as truly a fine art as poetry or painting; since it availed to communicate the mysteries to the human spirit.

The Children of the Pool

And perhaps, Mrs Morgan of Lanypwll Farm put all this much better in the speech of symbolism, when she murmured about the Children of the Pool. For if there is a landscape of sadness, there is certainly also a landscape of a horror of darkness and evil; and that black and oily depth, overshadowed with twisted woods, with its growth of foul weeds and its dead trees and leprous boughs, was assuredly potent in terror. To Roberts it was a strong drug, a drug of evocation; the black deep without calling to the black deep within, and summoning the inhabitant thereof to come forth. I made no attempt to extract the legend of that dark place from Mrs Morgan; and I do not suppose that she would have been communicative if I had questioned her. But it has struck me as possible and even probable that Roberts was by no means the first to experience the power of the pool.

Old stories often turn out to be true.

THE BRIGHT BOY

I

YOUNG JOSEPH LAST, having finally gone down from Oxford, wondered a good deal what he was to do next and for the years following next. He was an orphan from early boyhood, both his parents having died of typhoid within a few days of each other when Joseph was ten years old, and he remembered very little of Dunham, where his father ended a long line of solicitors, practising in the place since 1707. The Lasts had once been very comfortably off. They had intermarried now and again with the gentry of the neighbourhood and did a good deal of the county business, managing estates, collecting rents, officiating as stewards for several manors, living generally in a world of quiet but snug prosperity, rising to their greatest height, perhaps, during the Napoleonic Wars and afterwards. And then they began to decline, not violently at all, but very gently, so that it was many years before they were aware of the process that was going on, slowly, surely. Economists, no doubt, understand very well how the country and the country town gradually became less important soon after the Battle of Waterloo; and the causes of the decay and change which vexed Cobbett so sadly, as he saw, or thought he saw, the life and strength of the land being sucked up to nourish the monstrous excrescence of London. Anyhow, even before the railways came, the assembly rooms of the country towns grew dusty and desolate, the county families ceased to come to their town houses for the winter season, and the little theatres, where Mrs Siddons and Grimaldi had appeared in their divers parts, rarely opened their doors, and the skilled craftsmen, the clock-makers and the furniture-makers and the like began to drift away to the big towns and to the capital city. So it was with Dunham. Naturally the fortunes of the Lasts sank with the fortunes of the town; and there had been speculations which had not turned out well, and people spoke of a heavy loss in foreign bonds. When Joseph's father died, it was found that there was enough to educate the boy and keep him in strictly modest comfort and not much more.

He had his home with an uncle who lived at Blackheath, and after a few years at Mr Jones's well-known preparatory school, he went to Merchant Taylors and thence to Oxford. He took a decent degree (2nd in Greats) and then began that wondering process as to what he was to do with himself. His income would keep him in chops and steaks, with an occasional roast fowl, and three or four weeks on the Continent once a year. If he liked, he could do nothing, but the prospect seemed tame and boring. He was a very decent classical scholar, with something more than the average schoolmaster's purely technical knowledge of Latin and Greek and professional interest in them: still, schoolmastering seemed his only clear and obvious way of employing himself. But it did not seem likely that he would get a post at any of the big public schools. In the first place, he had rather neglected his opportunities at Oxford. He had gone to one of the obscurer colleges, one of those colleges which you may read about in memoirs dealing with the first years of the nineteenth century as centres and fountains of intellectual life; which for some reason or no reason have fallen into the shadow. There is nothing against them in any way; but nobody speaks of them any more. In one of these places Joseph Last made friends with good fellows, quiet and cheerful men like himself; but they were not, in the technical sense of the term, the 'good friends' which a prudent young man makes at the university. One or two had the bar in mind, and two or three the civil service; but most of them were bound for country curacies and country offices. Generally, and for practical purposes, they were 'out of it': they were not the men whose whispers could lead to anything profitable in high quarters. And then, again, even in those days, games were getting important in the creditable schools; and there, young Last was very decidedly out of it. He wore spectacles with lenses divided in some queer manner: his athletic disability was final and complete.

He pondered, and thought at first of setting up a small preparatory school in one of the well-to-do London suburbs; a day-school where parents might have their boys well grounded from the very beginning, for comparatively modest fees, and yet have their upbringing in their own hands. It had often struck Last that it was a barbarous business to send a little chap of seven or eight away from the comfortable and affectionate habit of his home to a strange place among cold strangers; to bare boards, an inky smell, and grammar on an empty stomach in the morning. But consulting with Jim Newman of his old college, he was warned by that sage to drop his scheme and leave it on the ground. Newman pointed out in the first place that there was no money in teaching unless it was combined with hotel-keeping. That, he said, was all right, and more than all right; and he surmised that many people who kept hotels in the ordinary way would give a good deal to practise their art and mystery under housemaster's rules. 'You needn't pay so very much for your furniture, you know. You don't want to make the boys into young sybarites. Besides, there's nothing a healthy-minded boy hates more than stuffiness: what he likes is clean fresh air and plenty of it. And, you know, old chap, fresh air is cheap enough. And then with the food, there's apt to be trouble in the ordinary hotel if it's uneatable; but in the sort of hotel we're talking of, a little accident with the beef or mutton affords a very valuable opportunity for the exercise of the virtue of self-denial.'

Last listened to all this with a mournful grin.

'You seem to know all about it,' he said. 'Why don't you go in for it yourself?'

'I couldn't keep my tongue in my cheek. Besides, I don't think it's fair sport. I'm going out to India in the autumn. What about pig-sticking?'

'And there's another thing,' he went on after a meditative pause. 'That notion of yours about a day prep school is rotten. The parents wouldn't say thank you for letting them keep their kids at home when they're all small and young. Some people go so far as to say that the chief purpose of schools is to allow parents a good excuse for getting rid of their children. That's nonsense. Most fathers and mothers are very fond of their children and like to have them about the house; when they're young, at all events. But somehow or other, they've got it into their heads that strange schoolmasters know more about bringing up a small boy than his own people; and there it is. So, on all counts, drop that scheme of yours.'

Last thought it over, and looked about him in the scholastic world, and came to the conclusion that Newman was right. For two or three years he took charge of reading parties in the long vacation. In the winter he found occupation in the coaching of backward boys, in preparing boys not so backward for scholarship examinations; and his little textbook, *Beginning Greek*, was found quite useful in lower school. He did pretty well on the whole, though the work began to bore him sadly, and such money as he earned, added to his income, enabled him to live in the way he liked, comfortably enough. He had a couple of rooms in one of the streets going down from the Strand to the river, for which he paid a pound a week, had bread and cheese and odds and ends for lunch, with beer from his own barrel in the cellar, and dined simply but sufficiently now in one, now in another of the snug taverns which then abounded in the quarter. And, now and again, once a month or so, perhaps, instead of the tavern dinners, there was the play at the Vaudeville or the Olympic, the Globe or the Strand, with supper and something hot to follow. The evening might turn into a little party: old Oxford friends would look him up in his rooms between six and seven; Zouch would gather from the Temple and Medwin from Buckingham Street, and possibly Garraway, taking the Yellow Albion bus, would descend from his remote steep in the northern parts of London, would knock at 14, Mowbray Street, and demand pipes, porter, and the pit at a good play. And, on rare occasions, another member of the little society, Noel, would turn up. Noel lived at Turnham Green in a red brick house which was then thought merely old-fashioned, which would now—but it was pulled down long ago—be distinguished as choice Queen Anne or Early Georgian. He lived there with his father, a retired official of the British Museum, and through a man whom he had known at Oxford, he had made some way in literary journalism, contributing regularly to an important weekly paper. Hence the consequence of his occasional descents on Buckingham Street, Mowbray Street, and the Temple. Noel, as in some sort a man of letters, or, at least, a professional journalist, was a member of Blacks' Club, which in those days had exiguous premises in

Maiden Lane. Noel would go round the haunts of his friends, and gather them to stout and oysters, and guide them into some neighbouring theatre pit, whence they viewed excellent acting and a cheerful, nonsensical play, enjoyed both, and were ready for supper at the Tavistock. This done, Noel would lead the party to Blacks', where they, very likely, saw some of the actors who had entertained them earlier in the evening, and Noel's friends, the journalists and men of letters, with a painter and a black-and-white man here and there. Here, Last enjoyed himself very much, more especially among the actors, who seemed to him more genial than the literary men. He became especially friendly with one of the players, old Meredith Mandeville, who had talked with the elder Kean, was reliable in the smaller Shakespearean parts, and had engaging tales to tell of early days in county circuits. 'You had nine shillings a week to begin with. When you got to fifteen shillings you gave your landlady eight or nine shillings, and had the rest to play with. You felt a prince. And the county families often used to come and see us in the Green Room: most agreeable.'

With this friendly old gentleman, whose placid and genial serenity was not marred at all by incalculable quantities of gin, Last loved to converse, getting glimpses of a life strangely remote from his own: vagabondage, insecurity, hard times, and jollity; and against it all as a background, the lighted murmur of the stage, voices uttering tremendous things, and the sense of moving in two worlds. The old man, by his own account, had not been eminently prosperous or successful, and yet he had relished his life, and drew humours from its disadvantages, and made hard times seem an adventure. Last used to express his envy of the player's career, dwelling on the dull insignificance of his own labours, which, he said, were a matter of tinkering small boys' brains, teaching older boys the tricks of the examiners, and generally doing things that didn't matter.

'It's no more education than bricklaying is architecture,' he said one night. 'And there's no fun in it.'

Old Mandeville, on his side, listened with interest to these revelations of a world as strange and unknown to him as the life of the floats was to the tutor. Broadly speaking, he knew nothing of any books but play books. He had heard, no doubt, of things called examinations, as most people have heard of Red Indian initiations; but to him one was as remote as the other. It was interesting and strange to him to be sitting at Blacks' and actually talking to a decent young fellow who was seriously engaged in this queer business. And there were—Last noted with amazement—points at which their two circles touched, or so it seemed. The tutor, wishing to be agreeable, began one night to talk about the origins of *King Lear*. The actor found himself listening to Celtic legends which to him sounded incomprehensible nonsense. And when it came to the Knight who fought the King of Fairyland for the hand of Cordelia till Doomsday, he broke in: 'Lear is a pill; there's no doubt of that. You're too young to have seen Barry O'Brien's Lear: magnificent. The part has been attempted since his day. But it has never been played. I have depicted the Fool myself, and, I must say, not without some meed of applause. I remember once at Stafford . . .' and Last was content to let him tell his tale, which ended, oddly enough, with a bullock's heart for supper.

But one night when Last was grumbling, as he often did, about the fragmentary, desultory, and altogether unsatisfactory nature of his occupation, the old man interrupted him in a wholly unexpected vein.

'It is possible,' he began, 'mark you, I say possible, that I may be the means of alleviating the tedium of your lot. I was calling some days ago on a cousin of mine, a Miss Lucy Pilliner, a very agreeable woman. She has a considerable knowledge of the world, and, I hope you will forgive the liberty, but I mentioned in the course of our conversation that I had lately became acquainted with a young gentleman of considerable scholastic distinction, who was somewhat dissatisfied with the too abrupt and frequent entrances and exits of his present tutorial employment. It struck me that my cousin received these remarks with a certain reflective interest, but I was not prepared to receive this letter.'

Mandeville handed Last the letter. It began: 'My dear Ezekiel,' and Last noted out of the corner of his eye a glance from the actor which pleaded for silence and secrecy on this point. The letter went on to say in a manner almost as dignified as Mandeville's, that the writer had been thinking over the circumstances of the young tutor, as related by her cousin in the course of their most agreeable conversation of Friday last, and she was inclined to think that she knew of an educational position shortly available in a private family, which would be of a more permanent and satisfactory nature. 'Should your friend feel interested,' Miss Pilliner ended, 'I should be glad if he would communicate with me, with a view to a meeting being arranged, at which the matter could be discussed with more exact particulars.'

'And what do you think of it?' said Mandeville, as Last returned Miss Pilliner's letter.

For a moment Last hesitated. There is an attraction and also a repulsion in the odd and the improbable, and Last doubted whether educational work obtained through an actor at Blacks' and a lady at Islington—he had seen the name at the top of the letter—could be altogether solid or desirable. But brighter thoughts prevailed, and he assured Mandeville that he would be only too glad to go thoroughly into the matter, thanking him very warmly for his interest. The old man nodded benignly, gave him the letter again that he might take down Miss Pilliner's address, and suggested an immediate note asking for an appointment.

'And now,' he said, 'despite the carping objections of the Moody Prince, I propose to drink your jocund health tonight.'

And he wished Last all the good luck in the world with hearty kindliness.

In a couple of days Miss Pilliner presented her compliments to Mr Joseph Last and begged him to do her the favour of calling on her on a date three days ahead, at noon, 'if neither day nor hour were in any way incompatible with his convenience. They might then, she proceeded, take advantage of the occasion to discuss a certain proposal, the nature of which, she believed, had been indicated to Mr Last by her good cousin, Mr Meredith Mandeville.

Corunna Square, where Miss Pilliner lived, was a small, almost a tiny, square in the remoter parts of Islington. Its two-storeyed houses of dim, yellowish brick were fairly covered with vines and clematis and all manner of creepers. In front of the houses were small paled gardens, gaily flowering, and the square enclosure held little else besides a venerable, wide-spreading mulberry, far older than the buildings about it. Miss Pilliner lived in the quietest corner of the square. She welcomed Last with some sort of compromise between a bow and a curtsy, and begged him to be seated in an upright armchair, upholstered in horse-hair. Miss Pilliner, he noted, looked about sixty, and was, perhaps, a little older. She was spare, upright, and composed; and yet one might have suspected a lurking whimsicality. Then, while the weather was discussed, Miss Pilliner offered a choice of port or sherry, sweet biscuits or plum cake. And so to the business of the day.

'My cousin, Mr Mandeville, informed me,' she began, 'of a young friend of great scholastic ability, who was, nevertheless, dissatisfied with the somewhat casual and occasional nature of his employment. By a singular coincidence, I had received a letter a day or two before from a friend of mine, a Mrs Marsh. She is, in fact, a distant connection, some sort of cousin, I suppose, but not being a Highlander or a Welshwoman, I really cannot say how many times removed. She was a lovely creature; she is still a handsome woman. Her name was Manning, Arabella Manning, and what possessed her to marry Mr Marsh I really cannot say. I only saw the man once, and I thought him her inferior in every respect, and considerably older. However, she declares that he is a devoted husband and an excellent person in every respect. They first met, odd as it must seem, in Pekin, where Arabella was governess in one of the legation families. Mr Marsh, I was given to understand, represented highly important commercial interests at the capital of the Flowery Land, and being introduced to my connection, a mutual attraction seems to have followed. Arabella Manning resigned her position in the attaché's family, and the marriage was solemnised in due course. I received this intelligence nine years ago in a letter from Arabella, dated at Pekin, and my relative ended by saying that she feared it would be impossible to furnish an address for an immediate reply, as Mr Marsh was about to set out on a mission of an extremely urgent nature on behalf of his firm, involving a great deal of travelling and frequent changes of address. I suffered a good deal of uneasiness on Arabella's account, it seemed such an unsettled way of life, and so unhomelike. However, a friend of mine who is in the City assured me that there was nothing unusual in the circumstances, and that there was no cause for alarm. Still, as the years went on, and I received no further communication from my cousin, I made up my mind that she had probably contracted some tropical disease which had carried her off, and that Mr Marsh had heartlessly neglected to communicate to me the intelligence of the sad event. But a month ago, almost to the day—Miss Pilliner referred to an almanac on the table beside her—I was astonished and delighted to receive a letter from Arabella. She wrote from one of the most luxurious and exclusive hotels in the West End of London, announcing the return of her husband and herself to their native land after many years of wandering. Mr Marsh's active concern in business had, it appeared, at length terminated in a highly prosperous and successful manner, and he was now in negotiation for the purchase of a small estate in the country, where he hoped to spend the remainder of his days in peaceful retirement.'

Miss Pilliner paused and replenished Last's glass.

'I am so sorry,' she continued, 'to trouble you with this long narrative, which, I am sure, must be a sad trial of your patience. But, as you will see presently, the circumstances are a little out of the common, and as you are, I trust, to have a particular interest in them, I think it is only right that you should be fully informed—fair and square, and all above board, as my poor father used to say in his bluff manner.

'Well, Mr Last, I received, as I have said, this letter from Arabella with its extremely gratifying intelligence. As you may guess, I was very much relieved to hear that all had turned out so felicitously. At the end of her letter,

Arabella begged me to come and see them at Billing's Hotel, saying that her husband was most anxious to have the pleasure of meeting me.'

Miss Pilliner went to a drawer in a writing-table by the window and took out a letter.

'Arabella was always considerate. She says: "I know that you have always lived very quietly, and are not accustomed to the turmoil of fashionable London. But you need not be alarmed. Billing's Hotel is no bustling modern caravanserai. Everything is very quiet, and, besides, we have our own small suite of apartments. Herbert—her husband, Mr Last—positively insists on your paying us a visit, and you must not disappoint us. If next Thursday, the 22nd, suits you, a carriage shall be sent at four o'clock to bring you to the hotel, and will take you back to Corunna Square, after you have joined us in a little dinner."

'Very kind, most considerate; don't you agree with me, Mr Last? But look at the postscript.'

Last took the letter, and read in a tight, neat script: 'PS. We have a wonderful piece of news for you. It is too good to write, so I shall keep it for our meeting.'

Last handed back Mrs Marsh's letter. Miss Pilliner's long and ceremonious approach was lulling him into a mild stupor; he wondered faintly when she would come to the point, and what the point would be like when she came to it, and, chiefly, what on earth this rather dull family history could have to do with him.

Miss Pilliner proceeded.

'Naturally, I accepted so kindly and urgent an invitation. I was anxious to see Arabella once more after her long absence, and I was glad to have the opportunity of forming my own judgment as to her husband, of whom I knew absolutely nothing. And then, Mr Last, I must confess that I am not deficient in that spirit of curiosity, which gentlemen have scarcely numbered with female virtues. I longed to be made partaker in the wonderful news which Arabella had promised to impart on our meeting, and I wasted many hours in speculating as to its nature.

'The day came. A neat brougham with its attendant footman arrived at the appointed hour, and I was driven in smooth luxury to Billing's Hotel in Manners Street, Mayfair. There a majordomo led the way to the suite of apartments on the first floor occupied by Mr and Mrs Marsh. I will not waste your valuable time, Mr Last, by expiating on the rich but quiet luxury of their apartments; I will merely mention that my relative assured me that the Sèvres ornaments in their drawing-room had been valued at nine hundred guineas. I found Arabella still a beautiful woman, but I could not help seeing that the tropical countries in which she had lived for so many years had taken their toll of her once resplendent beauty; there was a weariness, a lassitude in her appearance and demeanour which I was distressed to observe. As to her husband, Mr Marsh, I am aware that to form an unfavourable judgment after an acquaintance which has only lasted a few hours is both uncharitable and unwise; and I shall not soon forget the discourse which dear Mr Venn delivered at Emmanuel Church on the very Sunday after my visit to my relative: it really seemed, and I confess it with shame, that Mr Venn had my own case in mind, and felt it his bounden duty to warn me while it was yet time. Still, I must say that I did not take at all to Mr Marsh. I really can't say why. To me he was most polite; he could not have been more so. He remarked more than once on the extreme pleasure it gave him to meet at last one of whom he had heard so much from his dear Bella; he trusted that now his wandering days were over, the pleasure might be frequently repeated; he omitted nothing that the most genial courtesy might suggest. And yet, I cannot say that the impression I received was a favourable one. However; I dare say that I was mistaken.'

There was a pause. Last was resigned. The point of the long story seemed to recede into some far distance, into vanishing prospective.

'There was nothing definite?' he suggested.

'No; nothing definite. I may have thought that I detected a lack of candour, a hidden reserve behind all the generosity of Mr Marsh's expressions. Still; I hope I was mistaken.

'But I am forgetting in these trivial and I trust errone-ous observations, the sole matter that is of consequence; to you, at least, Mr Last. Soon after my arrival, before Mr Marsh had appeared, Arabella confided to me her great piece of intelligence. Her marriage had been blessed by offspring. Two years after her union with Mr Marsh, a child had been born, a boy. The birth took place at a town in South America, Santiago de Chile—I have verified the place in my atlas—where Mr Marsh's visit had been more protracted than usual. Fortunately, an English doctor was available, and the little fellow throve from the first, and as Arabella, his proud mother, boasted, was now a beautiful little boy, both handsome and intelligent to a remarkable degree. Naturally, I asked to see the child, but Arabella said that he was not in the hotel with them. After a few days it was thought that the dense and humid air of London was not suiting little Henry very well; and he had been sent with a nurse to a resort in the Isle of Thanet, where he was reported to be in the best of health and spirits.

'And now, Mr Last, after this tedious but necessary preamble, we arrive at that point where you, I trust, may be interested. In any case, as you may suppose, the life which the exigencies of business compelled the Marshes to lead, involving as it did almost continual travel, would have been little favourable to a course of systematic education for the child. But this obstacle apart, I gathered that Mr Marsh holds very strong views as to the folly of premature instruction. He declared to me his conviction that many fine minds had been grievously injured by being forced to undergo the process of early stimulation; and he pointed out that, by the nature of the case, those placed in charge of very young children were not persons of the highest acquirements and the keenest intelligence. "As you will readily agree, Miss Pilliner," he remarked to me, "great scholars are not employed to teach infants their alphabet, and it is not likely that the mysteries of the multiplication table will be imparted by a master of mathematics." In consequence, he urged, the young and budding intelligence is brought into contact with dull and inferior minds, and the damage may well be irreparable.'

There was much more, but gradually light began to dawn on the dazed man. Mr Marsh had kept the virgin intelligence of his son Henry undisturbed and uncorrupted by inferior and incompetent culture. The boy, it was judged, was now ripe for true education, and Mr and Mrs Marsh had begged Miss Pilliner to make enquiries, and to find, if she could, a scholar who would undertake the whole charge of little Henry's mental upbringing. If both parties were satisfied, the engagement would be for seven years at least, and the appointments, as Miss Pilliner called the salary, would begin with five hundred pounds a year, rising by an annual increment of fifty pounds. References, particulars of university distinctions would be required: Mr Marsh, long absent from England, was ready to proffer the names of his bankers. Miss Pilliner was quite sure, however, that Mr Last might consider himself engaged, if the position appealed to him.

Last thanked Miss Pilliner profoundly. He told her that he would like a couple of days in which to think the matter over. He would then write to her, and she would put him into communication with Mr Marsh. And so he went away from Corunna Square in a mood of great bewilderment and doubt. Unquestionably, the position had many advantages. The pay was very good. And he would be well lodged and well fed. The people were wealthy, and Miss Pilliner had assured him: 'You will have no cause to complain of your entertainment.' And from the educational point of view, it would certainly be an improvement on the work he had been doing since he left the university. He had been an odd-job man, a tinker, a patcher, a cobbler of other people's work; here was a chance to show that he was a master craftsman. Very few people, if any, in the teaching profession had ever enjoyed such an opportunity as this. Even the sixth-form masters in the big public schools must sometimes groan at having to underpin and relay the bad foundations of the fifth and fourth. He was to begin at the beginning, with no false work to hamper him: 'from A B C to Plato, Æschylus, and Aristotle,' he murmured to himself. Undoubtedly it was a big chance.

And on the other side? Well, he would have to give up London, and he had grown fond of the homely, cheerful London that he knew; his comfortable rooms in Mowbray Street, quiet enough down by the unfrequented Embankment, and yet but a minute or two from the ringing Strand. Then there were the meetings with the old Oxford friends, the nights at the theatre, the snug taverns with their curtained boxes, and their good chops and steaks and stout, and chimes of midnight and after, heard in cordial company at Blacks': all these would have to go. Miss Pilliner had spoken of Mr Marsh as looking for some place a considerable distance from town, 'in the real country'. He had his eye, she said, on a house on the Welsh border, which he thought of taking furnished, with the option of buying, if he eventually found it suited him. You couldn't look up old friends in London and get back the same night, if you lived somewhere on the Welsh border. Still, there would be the holidays, and a great deal might be done in the holidays.

And yet; there was still debate and doubt within his mind, as he sat eating his bread and cheese and potted meat, and drinking his beer in his sitting room in peaceful Mowbray Street. He was influenced, he thought, by Miss Pilliner's evident dislike of Mr Marsh, and though Miss Pilliner talked in the manner of Dr Johnson, he had a feeling that, like a lady of the Doctor's own day, she had a bottom of good sense. Evidently she did not trust Mr Marsh overmuch. Yet, what can the most cunning swindler do to his resident tutor? Give him cold mutton for dinner or forget to pay his salary? In either case, the remedy was simple: the resident tutor would swiftly cease to reside, and go back to London, and not be much the worse. After all, Last reflected, a man can't compel his son's tutor to invest in Uruguayan silver or Java spices or any other fallacious commercial undertaking, so what mattered the supposed trickiness of Marsh to him?

But again, when all had been summed up and considered, for and against; there was a vague objection remaining. To oppose this, Last could bring no argument, since it was without form of words, shapeless, and mutable as a cloud.

However, when the next morning came, there came with it a couple of letters inviting him to cram two young dunderheads with facts and figures and verbs in *mi*. The prospect was so terribly distasteful that he wrote to Miss Pilliner directly after breakfast, enclosing his college testimonials and certain other commendatory letters he had in his desk. In due course, he had an interview with Mr Marsh at Billing's Hotel. On the whole, each was well enough pleased with the other. Last found Marsh a lean, keen, dark man in later middle age; there was a grizzle in his black hair above the ears, and wrinkles seamed his face about the eyes. His eyebrows were heavy, and there was a hint of a threat in his jaw, but the smile with which he welcomed Last lit up his grimmish features into a genial warmth. There was an oddity about his accent and his tone in speaking; something foreign, perhaps? Last remembered that he had journeyed about the world for many years, and supposed that the echoes of many languages sounded in his speech. His manner and address were certainly suave, but Last had no prejudice against suavity, rather, he cherished a liking for the decencies of common intercourse. Still, no doubt, Marsh was not the kind of man Miss Pilliner was accustomed to meet in Corunna Square society or among Mr Venn's congregation. She probably suspected him of having been a pirate.

And Mr Marsh on his side was delighted with Last. As appeared from a letter addressed by him to Miss Pilliner—'or, may I venture to say, Cousin Lucy?'—Mr

The Bright Boy

Last was exactly the type of man he and Arabella had hoped to secure through Miss Pilliner's recommendation. They did not want to give their boy into the charge of a flashy man of the world with a substratum of learning. Mr Last was, it was evident, a quiet and unworldly scholar, more at home among books than among men; the very tutor Arabella and himself had desired for their little son. Mr Marsh was profoundly grateful to Miss Pilliner for the great service she had rendered to Arabella, to himself, and to Henry.

And, indeed, as Mr Meredith Mandeville would have said, Last looked the part. No doubt, the spectacles helped to create the remote, retired, Dominic Sampson impression.

In a week's time it was settled, he was to begin his duties. Mr Marsh wrote a handsome cheque, 'to defray any little matters of outfit, travelling expenses, and so forth; nothing to do with your salary'. He was to take the train to a certain large town in the west, and there he would be met and driven to the house, where Mrs Marsh and his pupil were already established—'beautiful country, Mr Last; I am sure you will appreciate it'.

There was a famous farewell gathering of the old friends. Zouch and Medwin, Garraway and Noel came from near and far. There was grilled sole before the mighty steak, and a roast fowl after it. They had decided that as it was the last time, perhaps, they would not go to the play, but sit and talk about the mahogany. Zouch, who was understood to be the ruler of the feast, had conferred with the head waiter, and when the cloth was removed, a rare and curious port was solemnly set before them. They talked of the old days when they were up at Wells together, pretended—though they knew better—that the undergraduate who had cut his own father in Piccadilly was a friend of theirs, retold jokes that must have been older than the wine, related tales of Moll and Meg, and the famous history of Melcombe, who screwed up the dean in his own rooms. And then there was the affair of the Poses Plastiques. Certain lewd fellows, as one of the dons of Wells College expressed it, had procured scandalous figures from the wax-work booth at the fair, and had disposed them by night about the fountain in the college garden in such a manner that their scandal was shamefully increased. The perpetrators of this infamy had never been discovered: the five friends looked knowingly at each other, pursed their lips, and passed the port.

The old wine and the old stories blended into a mood of gentle meditation; and then, at the right moment, Noel carried them off to Blacks' and new company. Last sought out old Mandeville and related, with warm gratitude, the happy issue of his intervention.

The chimes sounded, and they all went their several ways.

The Bright Boy

II

Though Joseph Last was by no means a miracle of observation and deduction, he was not altogether the simpleton among his books that Mr Marsh had judged him. It was not so very long before a certain uneasiness beset him in his new employment.

At first everything had seemed very well. Mr Marsh had been right in thinking that he would be charmed by the scene in which the White House was set. It stood, terraced on a hillside, high above a grey and silver river winding in esses through a lonely, lovely valley. Above it, to the east, was a vast and shadowy and ancient wood, climbing to the high ridge of the hill, and descending by height and by depth of green to the level meadows and to the sea. And, standing on the highest point of the wood above the White House, Last looked westward between the boughs and saw the lands across the river, and saw the country rise and fall in billow upon billow to the huge dim wall of the mountain, blue in the distance, and white farms shining in the sun on its vast side. Here was a man in a new world. There had been no such country as this about Dunham in the Midlands, or in the surroundings of Blackheath or Oxford; and he had visited nothing like it on his reading parties. He stood amazed, enchanted under the green shade, beholding a great wonder. Close beside him the well bubbled from the grey rocks, rising out of the heart of the hill.

And in the White House, the conditions of life were altogether pleasant. He had been struck by the dark beauty of Mrs Marsh, who was clearly, as Miss Pilliner had told him, a great many years younger than her husband. And he noted also that effect which her cousin had ascribed to years of living in the tropics, though he would hardly have called it weariness or lassitude. It was something stranger than that; there was the mark of flame upon her, but Last did not know whether it were the flame of the sun, or the stranger fires of places that she had entered, perhaps long ago.

But the pupil, little Henry, was altogether a surprise and a delight. He looked rather older than seven, but Last judged that this impression was not so much due to his height or physical make as to the bright alertness and intelligence of his glance. The tutor had dealt with many little boys, though with none so young as Henry; and he had found them as a whole a stodgy and podgy race, with faces that recorded a fixed abhorrence of learning and a resolution to learn as little as possible. Last was never surprised at this customary expression. It struck him as eminently natural. He knew that all elements are damnably dull and difficult. He wondered why it was inexorably appointed that the unfortunate human creature should pass a great portion of its life from the very beginning in doing things that it detested; but so it was, and now for the syntax of the optative.

But there were no such obstinate entrenchments in the face or the manner of Henry Marsh. He was a handsome boy, who looked brightly and spoke brightly, and evidently did not regard his tutor as a hostile force that had been brought against him. He was what some people would have called, oddly enough, old-fashioned; child-like, but not at all childish, with now and then a whimsical turn of phrase more suggestive of a humorous man than a little boy. This older habit was no doubt to be put down partly to the education of travel, the spectacle of the changing scene and the changing looks of men and things, but very largely to the fact that he had always been with his father and mother, and knew nothing of the company of children of his own age.

'Henry has had no playmates,' his father explained. 'He's had to be content with his mother and myself. It couldn't be helped. We've been on the move all the time; on shipboard or staying at cosmopolitan hotels for a few weeks, and then on the road again. The little chap had no chance of making any small friends.'

And the consequence was, no doubt, that lack of childishness that Last had noted. It was, probably, a pity that it was so. Childishness, after all, was a wonder world, and Henry seemed to know nothing of it: he had lost what might be, perhaps, as valuable as any other part of human experience, and he might find the lack of it as he grew older. Still, there it was; and Last ceased to think of these possibly fanciful deprivations, when he began to teach the boy, as he had promised himself, from the very beginning. Not quite from the beginning; the small boy confessed with a disarming grin that he had taught himself to read a little: 'But please, sir, don't tell my father, as I know he wouldn't like it. You see, my father and mother had to leave me alone sometimes, and it was so dull, and I thought it would be such fun if I learnt to read books all by myself.'

Here, thought Last, is a lesson for schoolmasters. Can learning be made a desirable secret, an excellent sport, instead of a horrible penance? He made a mental note, and set about the work before him. He found an extraordinary aptitude, a quickness in grasping his indications and explanations such as he had never known before—'not in boys twice his age, or three times his age, for the matter of that', as he reflected. This child, hardly removed from strict infancy, had something almost akin to genius—so the happy tutor was inclined to believe. Now and again, with his, 'Yes, sir, I see. And then, of course . . .' he would veritably take the coming words out of Last's mouth, and anticipate what was, no doubt, logically the next step in the demonstration. But Last had not been accustomed to pupils who anticipated anything— save the hour for putting the books back on the shelf. And above all, the instructor was captured by the eager and intense curiosity of the instructed. He was like a man reading *The Moonstone*, or some such sensational novel, and unable to put the book down till he had read to the very last page and found out the secret. This small boy brought just this spirit of insatiable curiosity to every subject put before him. 'I wish I had taught him to read,' thought Last to himself. 'I have no doubt he would have regarded the alphabet as we regard those entrancing and mysterious cyphers in Edgar Allan Poe's stories. And, after all, isn't that the right and rational way of looking at the alphabet?'

And then he went on to wonder whether curiosity, often regarded as a failing, almost a vice, is not, in fact, one of the greatest virtues of the spirit of man, the key to all knowledge and all the mysteries, the very sense of the secret that must be discovered.

With one thing and another: with this treasure of a pupil, with the enchantment of the strange and beautiful country about him, and with the extreme kindness and consideration shown him by Mr and Mrs Marsh, Last was in rich clover. He wrote to his friends in town, telling them of his happy experiences, and Zouch and Noel, meeting by chance at the Sun, the Dog, or the Triple Tun, discussed their friend's felicity.

'Proud of the pup,' said Zouch.

'And pleased with the prospect,' responded Noel, thinking of Last's lyrics about the woods and the waters, and the scene of the White House. 'Still, *timeo Hesperides et dona ferentes*. I mistrust the west. As one of its own people said, it is a land of enchantment and illusion. You never know what may happen next. It is a fortunate thing that Shakespeare was born within the safety line. If Stratford had been twenty or thirty miles farther west . . . I don't like to think of it. I am quite sure that only fairy gold is dug from Welsh gold-mines. And you know what happens to that.'

The Children of the Pool

Meanwhile, far from the lamps and rumours of the Strand, Last continued happy in his outland territory, under the great wood. But before long he received a shock. He was strolling in the terraced garden one afternoon between tea and dinner, his work done for the day; and feeling inclined for tobacco with repose, drifted towards the stone summer-house—or, perhaps, gazebo—that stood on the verge of the lawn in a coolness of dark ilex-trees. Here one could sit and look down on the silver winding of the river, crossed by a grey bridge of ancient stone. Last was about to settle down when he noticed a book on the table before him. He took it up, and glanced into it, and drew in his breath, and turning over a few more pages, sank aghast upon the bench. Mr Marsh had always deplored his ignorance of books. 'I knew how to read and write and not much more,' he would say, 'when I was thrown into business—at the bottom of the stairs. And I've been so busy ever since that I'm afraid it's too late now to make up for lost time.' Indeed, Last had noted that though Marsh usually spoke carefully enough, perhaps too carefully, he was apt to lapse in the warmth of conversation: he would talk of 'fax', meaning 'facts'. And yet, it seemed, he had not only found time for reading, but had acquired sufficient scholarship to make out the Latin of a terrible Renaissance treatise, not generally known even to collectors of such things. Last had heard of the book; and the few pages he had glanced at showed him that it thoroughly deserved its very bad character.

The Bright Boy

It was a disagreeable surprise. He admitted freely to himself that his employer's morals were no business of his. But why should the man trouble to tell lies? Last remembered queer old Miss Pilliner's account of her impressions of him; she had detected 'a lack of candour', something reserved behind a polite front of cordiality. Miss Pilliner was, certainly, an acute woman: there was an undoubted lack of candour about Marsh.

Last left the wretched volume on the summer-house table, and walked up and down the garden, feeling a good deal perturbed. He knew he was awkward at dinner, and said he felt a bit seedy, inclined to a headache. Marsh was bland and pleasant as usual, and Mrs Marsh sympathised with Last. She had hardly slept at all last night, she complained, and felt heavy and tired. She thought there was thunder in the air. Last, admiring her beauty, confessed again that Miss Pilliner had been right. Apart from her fatigue of the moment, there was a certain tropical languor about her, something of still, burning nights and the odour of strange flowers.

Marsh brought out a very special brandy which he administered with the black coffee; he said it would do both the invalids good, and that he would keep them company. Indeed, Last confessed to himself that he felt considerably more at ease after the good dinner, the good wine, and the rare brandy. It was humiliating, perhaps, but it was impossible to deny the power of the stomach. He went to his room early and tried to convince himself that the duplicity of Marsh was no affair of his. He found an innocent, or almost innocent explanation of it before he had finished his last pipe, sitting at the open window, hearing faintly the wash of the river and gazing towards the dim lands beyond it.

'Here,' he meditated, 'we have a modified form of Bounderby's Disease. Bounderby said that he began life as a wretched, starved, neglected little outcast. Marsh says that he was made into an office boy or something of the sort before he had time to learn anything. Bounderby lied, and no doubt Marsh lies. It is the trick of wealthy men; to magnify their late achievements by magnifying their early disadvantages.'

By the time he went to sleep he had almost decided that the young Marsh had been to a good grammar school, and had done well.

The next morning, Last awoke almost at ease again. It was no doubt a pity that Marsh indulged in a subtle and disingenuous form of boasting, and his taste in books was certainly deplorable: but he must look after that himself. And the boy made amends for all. He showed so clean a grasp of the English sentence, that Last thought he might well begin Latin before very long. He mentioned this one night at dinner, looking at Marsh with a certain humorous intention. But Marsh gave no sign that the dart had pricked him.

'That shows I was right,' he remarked. 'I've always said there's no greater mistake than forcing learning on children before they're fit to take it in. People will do it, and in nine cases out of ten the children's heads are muddled for the rest of their lives. You see how it is with Henry; I've kept him away from books up to now, and you see for yourself that I've lost him no time. He's ripe for learning, and I shouldn't wonder if he got ahead better in six months than the ordinary, early-crammed child would in six years.'

It might be so, Last thought, but on the whole he was inclined to put down the boy's swift progress rather to his own exceptional intelligence than to his father's system, or no system. And in any case, it was a great pleasure to teach such a boy. And his application to his books had certainly no injurious effect on his spirits. There was not much society within easy reach of the White House, and, besides, people did not know whether the Marshes were to settle down or whether they were transient visitors: they were chary of paying their calls while there was this uncertainty. However, the rector had called; first of all the rector and his wife, she cheery, good-humoured and chatty; he somewhat dim and vague. It was understood that the rector, a high wrangler in his day, divided his time between his garden and the invention of a flying machine. He had the character of being slightly eccentric. He came not again, but Mrs Winslow would drive over by the forest road in the governess car with her two children; Nancy, a pretty fair girl of seventeen, and Ted, a boy of eleven or twelve, of that type which Last catalogued as 'stodgy and podgy', broad and thick set, with bulgy cheeks and eyes, and something of the determined expression of a young bulldog. After tea Nancy would organise games for the two boys in the garden and join in them herself with apparent relish. Henry, who had known few companions besides his parents, and had probably never played a game of any kind, squealed with delight, ran here and there and everywhere, hid behind the summer-house and popped out from the screen of the French beans with the greatest gusto, and Ted Winslow joined in with an air of protest. He was on his holidays, and his expression signified that all that sort of thing was only fit for girls and kids. Last was delighted to see Henry so ready and eager to be amused; after all, he had something of the child in him. He seemed a little uncomfortable when Nancy Winslow took him on her knee after the sports were over; he was evidently fearful of Ted Winslow's scornful eye. Indeed, the young bulldog looked as if he feared that his character would be compromised by associating with so manifest and confessed a kid. The next time Mrs Winslow took tea at the White House, Ted had a diplomatic headache and stayed at home. But Nancy found games that two could play, and she and Henry were heard screaming with joy all over the gardens. Henry wanted to show Nancy a wonderful well that he had discovered in the forest; it came, he said, from under the roots of a great yew-tree. But Mrs Marsh seemed to think that they might get lost.

Last had got over the uncomfortable incident of that villainous book in the summer-house. Writing to Noel, he had remarked that he feared his employer was a bit of an old rascal in some respects, but all right so far as he was

concerned; and there it was. He got on with his job and
minded his own business. Yet, now and again, his doubt-
ful uneasiness about the man was renewed. There was a
bad business at a hamlet a couple of miles away, where a
girl of twelve or thirteen, coming home after dusk from a
visit to a neighbour, had been set on in the wood and very
vilely misused. The unfortunate child, it would appear,
had been left by the scoundrel in the black dark of the
forest, at some distance from the path she must have
taken on her way home. A man who had been drinking
late at the Fox and Hounds heard crying and screaming,
'like someone in a fit', as he expressed it, and found the
girl in a terrible state, and in a terrible state she had
remained ever since. She was quite unable to describe the
person who had so shamefully maltreated her; the shock
had left her beside herself; she cried out once that something had come behind her in the dark, but she could say
no more, and it was hopeless to try to get her to describe
a person that, most likely, she had not even seen. Naturally, this very horrible story made something of a feature
in the local paper, and one night, as Last and Marsh were
sitting smoking after dinner, the tutor spoke of the affair;
said something about the contrast between the peace and
beauty and quiet of the scene and the villainous crime that
had been done hard by. He was surprised to find that
Marsh grew at once ill at ease. He rose from his chair and
walked up and down the room, muttering 'horrible business, shameful business'; and when he sat down again,
with the light full on him, Last saw the face of a fright-

ened man. The hand that Marsh laid on the table was twitching uneasily; he beat with his foot on the floor as he tried to bring his lips to order, and there was a dreadful fear in his eyes.

Last was shocked and astonished at the effect he had produced with a few conventional phrases. Nervously, willing to tide over a painful situation, he began to utter something even more conventional to the effect that the loveliness of external nature had never conferred immunity from crime, or some stuff to the same inane purpose. But Marsh, it was clear, was not to be soothed by anything of the kind. He started again from his chair and struck his hand upon the table, with a fierce gesture of denial and refusal.

'Please, Mr Last, let it be. Say no more about it. It has upset Mrs Marsh and myself very much indeed. It horrifies us to think that we have brought our boy here, to this peaceful place as we thought, only to expose him to the contagion of this dreadful affair. Of course we have given the servants strict orders not to say a word about it in Henry's presence; but you know what servants are, and what very sharp ears children have. A chance word or two may take root in a child's mind and contaminate his whole nature. It is, really, a very terrible thought. You must have noticed how distressed Mrs Marsh has been for the last few days. The only thing we can do is to try and forget it all, and hope no harm has been done.'

Last murmured a word or two of apology and agreement, and the talk moved off into safer country. But

114

when the tutor was alone, he considered what he had seen and heard very curiously.

He thought that Marsh's looks did not match his words. He spoke as the devoted father, afraid that his little boy should overhear nauseous and offensive gossip and conjecture about a horrible and obscene crime. But he looked like a man who had caught sight of a gallows, and that, Last felt, was altogether a very different kind of fear. And, then, there was his reference to his wife. Last had noticed that since the crime in the forest there had been something amiss with her; but, again, he mistrusted Marsh's comment. Here was a woman whose usual habit was a rather lazy good humour; but of late there had been a look and an air of suppressed fury, the burning glance of a jealous woman, the rage of despised beauty. She spoke little, and then as briefly as possible; but one might suspect flames and fires within. Last had seen this and wondered, but not very much, being resolved to mind his own business. He had supposed there had been some difference of opinion between her and her husband; very likely about the rearrangement of the drawing-room furniture and hiring a grand piano. He certainly had not thought of tracing Mrs Marsh's altered air to the villainous crime that had been committed. And now Marsh was telling him that these glances of concealed rage were the outward signs of tender maternal anxiety; and not one word of all that did he believe. He put Marsh's half-hidden terror beside his wife's half-hidden fury; he thought of the book in the summer-house and things that were being whispered about the horror in the wood: and loathing and dread possessed him. He had no proof, it was true; merely conjecture, but he felt no doubt. There could be no other explanation. And what could he do but leave this terrible place?

Last could get no sleep. He undressed and went to bed, and tossed about in the half dark of the summer night. Then he lit his lamp and dressed again, and wondered whether he had better not steal away without a word, and walk the eight miles to the station, and escape by the first train that went to London. It was not merely loathing for the man and his works; it was deadly fear, also, that urged him to fly from the White House. He felt sure that if Marsh guessed at his suspicions of the truth, his life might well be in danger. There was no mercy or scruple in that evil man. He might even now be at his door, listening, waiting. There was cold terror in his heart, and cold sweat pouring at the thought. He paced softly up and down his room in his bare feet, pausing now and again to listen for that other soft step outside. He locked the door as silently as he could, and felt safer. He would wait till the day came and people were stirring about the house, and then he might venture to come out and make his escape.

And yet when he heard the servants moving over their work, he hesitated. The light of the sun was shining in the valley, and the white mist over the silver river floated upward and vanished; the sweet breath of the wood entered the window of his room. The black horror and fear were raised from his spirit. He began to hesitate, to suspect his judgement, to inquire whether he had not rushed to his black conclusions in a panic of the night. His logical deductions at midnight seemed to smell of nightmare in the brightness of that valley; the song of the aspiring lark confuted him. He remembered Garraway's great argument after a famous supper at the Turk's Head: that it was always unsafe to make improbability the guide of life. He would delay a little, and keep a sharp look out, and be sure before taking sudden and violent action. And perhaps the truth was that Last was influenced very strongly by his aversion from leaving young Henry, whose extraordinary brilliance and intelligence amazed and delighted him more and more.

It was still early when at last he left his room, and went out into the pure morning air. It was an hour or more before breakfast time, and he set out on the path that led past the wall of the kitchen garden up the hill and into the heart of the wood. He paused a moment at the upper corner, and turned round to look across the river at the happy country showing its morning magic and delight. As he dawdled and gazed, he heard soft steps approaching on the other side of the wall, and low voices murmuring. Then, as the steps drew near, one of the voices was raised a little, and Last heard Mrs Marsh speaking:

'Too old, am I? And thirteen is too young. Is it to be seventeen next when you can get her into the wood? And after all I have done for you, and after what you have done to me.'

Mrs Marsh enumerated all these things without remission, and without any quiver of shame in her voice. She paused for a moment. Perhaps her rage was choking her; and there was a shrill piping cackle of derision, as if Marsh's voice had cracked in its contempt.

Very softly, but very swiftly, Last, the man with the grey face and the staring eyes, bolted for his life, down and away from the White House. Once in the road, free from the fields and brakes, he changed his run into a walk, and he never paused or stopped, till he came with a gulp of relief into the ugly streets of the big industrial town. He made his way to the station at once, and found that he was an hour too soon for the London express. So there was plenty of time for breakfast; which consisted of brandy.

III

The tutor went back to his old life and his old ways, and did his best to forget the strange and horrible interlude of the White House. He gathered his podgy pups once more about him; crammed and coached, read with undergraduates during the long vacation, and was moderately satisfied with the course of things in general. Now and then, when he was endeavouring to persuade the podges against their deliberate judgement that Latin and Greek were languages once spoken by human beings, not senseless enigmas invented by demons, he would think with a sigh of regret of the boy who understood and longed to understand. And he wondered whether he had not been a coward to leave that enchanting child to the evil mercies of his hideous parents. But what could he have done? But it was dreadful to think of Henry, slowly or swiftly corrupted by his detestable father and mother, growing up with the fat slime of their abominations upon him.

He went into no detail with his old friends. He hinted that there had been grave unpleasantness, which made it impossible for him to remain in the west. They nodded, and perceiving that the subject was a sore one, asked no questions, and talked of old books and the new steak instead. They all agreed, in fact, that the steak was far too new, and William was summoned to explain this horror. Didn't he know that beefsteak, beefsteak meant for the consumption of Christian men, as distinguished from Hottentots, required hanging just as much as game? William, the ponderous and benignant, tasted and tested, and agreed; with sorrowful regret. He apologised, and went on to say that as the gentlemen would not care to wait for a fowl, he would suggest a very special, tender, and juicy fillet of roast veal, then in cut. The suggestion was accepted, and found excellent. The conversation turned to Choric metres and Florence St John at the Strand. There was port later.

It was many years afterwards, when this old life, after crumbling for a long while, had come down with a final crash, that Last heard the real story of his tutorial engagement at the White House. Three dreadful people were put in the dock at the Old Bailey. There was an old man, with the look of a deadly snake; a fat, sloppy, deplorable woman with pendulous cheeks and a faint hint of perished beauty in her eyes; and to the utter blank amazement of those who did not know the story, a wonderful little boy. The people who saw him in court said he might have been taken for a child of nine or ten; no more. But the evidence that was given showed that he must be between fifty and sixty at the least; perhaps more than that.

The indictment charged these three people with an unspeakable and hideous crime. They were charged under the name of Mailey, the name which they had borne at the time of their arrest; but it turned out at the end of the trial that they had been known by many names in the course of their career: Mailey, Despasse, Lartigan, Delarue, Falcon, Lecossic, Hammond, Marsh, Haringworth. It was established that the apparent boy, whom Last had known as Henry Marsh, was no relation of any kind to the elder prisoners. 'Henry's' origins were deeply obscure. It was conjectured that he was the illegitimate son of a very high Englishman, a diplomatist, whose influence had counted for a great deal in the Far East. Nobody knew anything about the mother. The boy showed brilliant promise from very early years, and the father, a bachelor, and disliking what little he knew of his relations, left his very large fortune to his son. The diplomatist died when the boy was twelve years old; and he had been aged, and more than aged when the child was born. People remarked that Arthur Wesley, as he was then called, was very short for his years, and he remained short, and his face remained that of a boy of seven or eight. He could not be sent to a school, so he was privately educated. When he was of age, the trustees had the extraordinary experience of placing a very considerable property in the hands of a young man who looked like a little boy. Very soon afterwards, Arthur Wesley disappeared. Dubious rumours spoke of reappearances, now here, now there, in all quarters of the world. There were tales that he had 'gone fantee' in what was then unknown Africa, when the Mountains of the Moon still lingered on the older maps. It was reported, again, that he had gone exploring in the higher waters of the Amazon, and had never come back; but a few years later a personage that must have been Arthur Wesley was displaying unpleasant activities in Macao. It was soon after this period, according to the prosecution, that—in the words of counsel—he realised the necessity of 'taking cover'. His extraordinary personality, naturally enough, drew attention to him and his doings, and these doings being generally or always of an infamous kind, such attention was both inconvenient and dangerous. Somewhere in the East, and in very bad company, he came upon the two people who were charged with him. Arabella Manning, who was said to have respectable connections in Wiltshire, had gone out to the East as a governess, but had soon found other occupations. Meers had been a clerk in a house of business at Shanghai. His very ingenious system of fraud obtained his discharge, but, for some reason or other, the firm refused to prosecute, and Meers went—where Arthur Wesley found him. Wesley thought of his great plan. Manning and Meers were to pretend to be Mr and Mrs Marsh—that seemed to have been their original style—and he was to be their little boy. He paid them well for their various services: Arabella was his mistress-in-chief, the companion of his milder moments, for some years. Occasionally, a tutor was engaged to make the situation more plausible. In this state, the horrible trio peregrinated over the earth.

The court heard all this, and much more, after the jury had found the three prisoners guilty of the particular offence with which they were charged. This last crime—which the press had to enfold in paraphrase and periphrase—had been discovered, strange as it seemed, largely as a result of the woman's jealousy. Wesley's—affections, let us call them, were still apt to wander, and Arabella's jealous rage drove her beyond all caution and all control. She was the weak joint in Wesley's armour, the rent in his cover. People in court looked at the two; the debauched, deplorable woman with her flagging, sagging cheeks, and the dim fire still burning in her weary old eyes, and at Wesley, still, to all appearance, a bright and handsome little boy; they gasped with amazement at the grotesque, impossible horror of the scene. The judge raised his head from his notes, and gazed steadily at the convicted persons for some moments; his lips were tightly compressed.

The detective drew to the end of his portentous history. The track of these people, he said, had been marked by many terrible scandals, but till quite lately there had been no suspicion of their guilt. Two of these cases involved the capital charge, but formal evidence was lacking.

He drew to his close.

'In spite of his diminutive stature and juvenile appearance, the prisoner, Charles Mailey, *alias* Arthur Wesley, made a desperate resistance to his arrest. He is possessed of immense strength for his size, and almost choked one of the officers who arrested him.'

The formulas of the court were uttered. The judge, without a word of comment, sentenced Mailey, or Wesley, to imprisonment for life, John Meers to fifteen years' imprisonment, Arabella Manning to ten years' imprisonment.

The old world, it has been noted, had crashed down. Many, many years had passed since Last had been hunted out of Mowbray Street, that went down dingily, peacefully from the Strand. Mowbray Street was now all blazing office buildings. Later, he had been driven from one nook and corner and snug retreat after another as new London rose in majesty and splendour. But for a year or more he had lain hidden in a by-street that had the advantage of leading into a disused graveyard near the

Gray's Inn Road. Medwin and Garraway were dead; but Last summoned the surviving Zouch and Noel to his abode one night; and then and there made punch, and good punch for them.

'It's so jolly it must be sinful,' he said, as he pared his lemons, 'but up to the present I believe it is not illegal. And I still have a few bottles of that port I bought in ninety-two.'

And then he told them for the first time all the whole story of his engagement at the White House.

The Tree of Life

THE MORGANS of Llantrisant were regarded for many centuries as among the most considerable of the landed gentry of South Wales. They had been called Reformation *parvenus,* but this was a piece of unhistorical and unjust abuse. They could trace their descent back, without doubt, certainly as far as Morgan ab Ifor, who fought and, no doubt, flourished in his way *c.*980. He, in his turn, was always regarded as of the tribe of St Teilo; and the family kept, as a most precious relic, a portable altar which was supposed to have belonged to the saint. And for many hundred years, the eldest son had borne the name of Teilo. They had intermarried, now and again, with the Normans, and lived in a thirteenth-century castle, with certain additions for comfort and amenity made in the reign of Henry VII, whose cause they had supported with considerable energy. From Henry, they had received grants of forfeited estates, both in Monmouthshire and Glamorganshire. At the dissolution of the religious houses, the Sir Teilo of the day was given Llantrisant Abbey with all its possessions. The monastic church was stripped of its lead roof, and soon fell into ruin, and became a quarry for the neighbourhood. The abbot's lodging and other of the monastic buildings were kept in repair, and being situated in a sheltered valley, were used by the family as a winter residence in preference to the castle, which was on a bare hill, high above the abbey. In the seventeenth century, Sir Henry Morgan—his elder brother had died young—was a Parliament man. He changed his opinions, and rose for the King in 1648; and, in consequence, had the mortification of seeing the outer wall of the castle on the hill, not razed to the ground, but carefully reduced to a height of four or five feet by the Cromwellian major-general commanding in the west. Later in the century, the Morgans became Whigs, and later still were able to support Mr Gladstone, up to the Home Rule Bill of 1886. They still held most of the lands which they had gathered together gradually for eight or nine hundred years. Many of these lands had been wild, remote, and mountainous, of little use or profit save for the sport of hunting the hare; but early in the nineteenth century mining experts from the north, Fothergills and Renshaws, had found coal, and pits were sunk in the wild places, and the Morgans became wealthy in the modern way. By consequence, the bad seasons of the late 'seventies and the agricultural depression of the early 'eighties hardly touched them. They reduced rents and remitted arrears and throve on their mining royalties: they were still great people of the county. It was a very great pity that Teilo Morgan of Llantrisant was an invalid and an enforced recluse; especially as he was devoted to the memories of his house, and to the estate, and to the interests of the people on it.

The Llantrisant Abbey of his day had been so altered from age to age that the last abbot would certainly have seen little that was familiar to his eyes. It was set in rich and pleasant meadow-land, with woods of oak and beech and ash and elm all about it. Through the park ran the swift, clear river, Avon Torfaen, the stone or boulder-crusher, so named from its furious courses in the mountains where it rose. And the hills stood round the Abbey on every side. Here and there in the southern-facing front of the house, there could be seen traces of fifteenth-century building; but on this had been imposed the Elizabethan gables of the first lay resident, and Inigo Jones was said to have added the brick wing with the Corinthian pilasters, and there was a stuccoed projection in the sham Gothic of the time of George II. It was architecturally ridiculous but it was supposed to be the warmest part of the house, and Teilo Morgan occupied a set of five or six rooms on the first floor, and often looked out on the park, and opened the windows to hear the sound of the pouring Avon, and the murmur of the wood-pigeons in the trees, and the noise of the west wind from the mountain. He longed to be out among it all, running as he saw boys running on the hill-side through a gap in the wood; but he knew that there was a gulf fixed between him and that paradise. There was, it seemed, no specific disease but a profound weakness, a *marasmus* that had stopped short of its term, but kept the patient chronically incapable of any physical exertion, even the slightest. They had once tried taking him out on a very fine day in the park, in a wheeled chair; but even that easy motion was too much for him. After ten minutes, he had fainted, and lay for two or three days on his back, alive, but little more than alive. Most of his time was spent on a couch. He would sit up for his meals and to interview the estate agent; but it was effort to do so much as this. He used to read in county histories and in old family records of the doings of his ancestors; and wonder what they would have said to such a successor. The storming of castles at dead darkness of night, the firing of them so that the mountains far away shone, the arrows of the Gwent bowmen darkening the air at Crècy, the battle of the dawn by the river, when it was seen scarlet by the first light in the east, the drinking of Gascon wine in hall from moonrise to sunrise: he was no figure for the old days and works of the Morgans.

It was probable that his feeble life was chiefly sustained by his intense interest in the doings of the estate. The agent, Captain Vaughan, a keen, middle-aged man, had often told him that a monthly interview would be sufficient and more than sufficient. 'I'm afraid you find all this detail terribly tiring,' he would say. 'And you know it's not really necessary. I've one or two good men under me, and between us we manage to keep things in very decent order. I do assure you, you needn't bother. As a matter of fact; if I brought you a statement once a quarter, it would be quite enough.'

But Teilo Morgan would not entertain any such laxity.

'It doesn't tire me in the least,' he always replied to the agent's remonstrances. 'It does me good. You know a man must have exercise in some form or another. I get mine on your legs. I'm still enjoying that tramp of yours up to Castell-y-Bwch three years ago. You remember?'

Captain Vaughan seemed at a loss for a moment.

'Let me see,' he said. 'Three years ago? Castell-y-Bwch? Now, what was I doing up there?'

'You can't have forgotten. Don't you recollect? It was just after the great snowstorm. You went up to see that the roof was all right, and fell into a fifteen-foot drift on the way.'

'I remember now,' said Vaughan. 'I should think I do remember. I don't think I've been so cold and so wet before or since—worse than the Balkans. I wasn't pre-pared for it. And when I got through the snow, there was an infernal mountain stream still going strong beneath it all.'

'But there was a good fire at the pub when you got there?'

'Half-way up the chimney; coal and wood mixed; roaring, I've never seen such a blaze: six foot by three, I should think. And I told them to mix it strong.'

'I wish I'd been there,' said the squire. 'Let me see; you recommended that some work should be done on the place, didn't you? Re-roofing, wasn't it?'

'Yes, the slates were in a bad way, and in the following March we replaced them by stone tiles, extra heavy. Slates are not good enough, half-way up the mountain. To the west, of course, the place is more or less protected by the wood, but the south-east pine end is badly exposed and was letting the wet through, so I ran up an oak frame, nine inches from the wall, and fixed tiles on that. You remember passing the estimate?'

'Of course, of course. And it's done all right? No trouble since?'

'No trouble with wind or weather. When I was there last, the fat daughter was talking about going to service in Cardiff. I don't think Mrs Samuel fancied it much. And young William wants to go down the pit when he leaves school.'

'Thomas is staying to help his father with the farm, I hope? And how is the farm doing now?'

'Fairly well. They pay their rent regularly, as you know. In spite of what I tell them, they will try to grow wheat. It's much too high up.'

'How do the people on the mountain like the new parson?'

'They get on with him all right. He tries to persuade them to come to Mass, as he calls it, and they stay away and go to meeting. But quite on friendly terms—out of business hours.'

'I see. I should think he would be more at home in one of the Cardiff parishes. We must see if it can't be worked somehow. And how about those new pigsties at Ty,

Captain? Have you got the estimate with you? Read it out, will you? My eyes are tired this morning. You went to Davies for the estimate? That's right: the policy of the estate is, always encourage the small man. Have you looked into that business of the marsh?'

'The marsh? Oh, you mean at Kemeys? Yes, I've gone into it. But I don't think it would pay for draining. You'd never see your money back.'

'You think not? That's a pity.'

Teilo Morgan seemed depressed by the agent's judgment on the Kemeys marshland. He weighed the matter.

'Well; I suppose you are right. We mustn't go in for fancy farming. But look here! It's just struck me. Why not utilise the marsh for growing willows? We could run a sluice from the brook right across it. It might be possible to start basket-making—in a small way, of course, at first. What do you think?'

'That wants looking into,' said Captain Vaughan. 'I know a place in Somerset where they are doing something of the kind. I'll go over on Wednesday and see if I can get some useful information. I hardly think the margin of profit would be a big one. But you would be satisfied with two per cent?'

'Certainly. And here's a thing I've been wanting to talk to you about for a long time—for the last three or four Mondays—and I've always forgotten. You know the Graeg on the home farm? A beautiful southern exposure, and practically wasted. I feel sure that egg-plants would do splendidly there. Could you manage to get out some figures for next Monday? There's no reason why the egg-plant shouldn't become as popular as the tomato and the banana; if a cheap supply were forthcoming. You will see to that, won't you? If you're busy, you might put off going to Somerset till next week: no hurry about the marsh.'

'Very good. The Graeg: egg-plants.' The agent made an entry in his note-book, and took his leave soon afterwards. He paced a long corridor till he came to the gallery, from which the main staircase of the Abbey went down to the entrance hall. There he encountered an important-looking personage, square-chinned, black-coated, slightly grizzled.

'As usual, I suppose?' the personage enquired.

'As usual.'

'What was it this time?'

'Egg-plants.'

The important one nodded, and Captain Vaughan went on his way.

II

As soon as the agent had gone, Teilo Morgan rang a bell. His man came, and lifted him skilfully out of the big chair, and laid him on the day-bed by the window, propping him with cushions behind his back.

'Two cushions will be enough,' said the squire. 'I'm rather tired this morning.'

The Tree of Life

The man put the bell within easy reach, and went out softly. Teilo Morgan lay back quite still; thinking of old days, and of happy years, and of the bad season that followed them. His first recollections were of a little cottage, snow-white, high upon the mountain, a little higher than the hamlet of Castell-y-Bwch, of which he had been talking to the agent. The shining walls of the cottage, freshly whitened every Easter, were very thick, and sloped outward to the ground: the windows were deep-set in the wall. By the porch which sheltered the front door from the great winds of the mountain, were two shrubs, one on each side, that were covered in their season with orange-coloured flowers, as round as oranges, and these golden flowers were, in his memory, tossed and shaken to and fro, in the breeze that always blew in that high land, when every leaf and blossom of the lower slopes were still. About the house was the garden, and a rough field, and a small cherry orchard, in a sheltered dip of land, and a well dripping from the grey rock with water very clear and cold. Above the cottage and its small demesne came a high bank, with a hedge of straggling, wind-beaten trees and bramble thickets on top of it, and beyond, the steep and wild ascent of the mountain, where the dark green whin bushes bore purple berries, where white cotton grew on the grass, and the bracken shimmered in the sun, and the imperial heather glowed on golden autumn days. Teilo remembered well how, a long age ago, he would stand in summer weather by the white porch, and look down on the great territory, as if on the whole world, far below: wave following wave of hill and valley, of dark wood and green pastures and cornfields, pale green or golden, the white farms shining, the mist of blue smoke above the Roman city, and to the right, the far waters of the yellow sea. And then there were the winter nights: all the air black as pitch, and a noise of tumult and battle, when the great winds and driving rain beat upon wall and window; and it was praise and thanksgiving to lie safe and snug in a cot by the settle near the light and the warmth of the fire, while without the heavens and the hills were confounded together in the roaring darkness.

In the white cottage on the high land, Teilo had lived with his mother and grandmother, very old, bent and wrinkled; with a sallow face, and hair still black in spite of long years. But he was a very small boy, when a gentleman who had often been there before, came and took his mother and himself away, down into the valley; and his next memories were of the splendours of Llantrisant Abbey, where the three of them lived together, and were waited on by many servants, and he found that the gentleman was his father: a cheerful man, always laughing, with bright blue eyes and a thick, tawny moustache, that drooped over his chin. Here Teilo ran about the park, and; raced sticks in the racing Avon, and climbed up the steep hill they called the Graeg, and liked to be there because with the shimmering, sweet-scented bracken it was like the mountain-side. His walks and runs and climbs did not last long. The strange illness that nobody

134

seemed to understand struck him down, and when after many weeks of bitter pains and angry, fiery dreams, the anguish of day and night left him; he was weak and helpless, and lay still, waiting to get well, and never got well again. Month after month he lay there in his bed, able to move his hands faintly, and no more. At the end of a year he felt a little stronger and tried to walk, and just managed to get across the room, helping himself from chair to chair. There was one thing that was for the better: he had been a silent child, happy to sit all by himself hour after hour on the mountain and then on the steep slope of the Graeg, without uttering a word or wanting anyone to come and talk to him. Now, in his weakness, he chattered eagerly, and thought of admirable things. He would tell his father and mother all the schemes and plans he was making, and he wondered why they looked so sadly at him.

And then, disaster. His father died, and his mother and he had to leave Llantrisant Abbey; they never told him why. They went to live in a grey, dreary street somewhere in the north of London. It was a place full of ugly sights and sounds, with a stench of burning bones always in the heavy air, and an unseemly litter of egg-shells and torn paper and cabbage-stalks about the gutters, and screams and harsh cries fouling the ears at midnight. And in winter, the yellow sulphur mist shut out the sky and burned sourly in the nostrils. A dreadful place, and the exile was long there. His mother went out on most days soon after breakfast, and often did not come back till ten, eleven, twelve at night, tired to death, as she said, and her dark beauty all marred and broken. Two or three times, in the course of the day, a neighbour from the floor below would come in and see if he wanted anything; but, except for these visits, he lay alone all the hours, and read in the few old books that they had in the room. It was a life of bewildered misery. There was not much to eat, and what there was seemed not to have the right taste or smell; and he could not understand why they should have to live in the horrible street, since his mother had told him that now his father was dead, he was the rightful master of Llantrisant Abbey and should be a very rich man. 'Then why are we in this dreadful place?' he asked her; and she only cried.

And then his mother died. And a few days after the funeral, people came and took him away; and he found himself once more at Llantrisant, master of it all, as his mother had told him he should be. He made up his mind to learn all about the lands and farms that he owned, and got them to bring him the books of the estate, and then Captain Vaughan began to come and see him, and tell him how things were going on, and how this farmer was the best tenant in the county, and how that man had nothing but bad luck, and John Williams would put gin in his cider, and drive breakneck down steep, stony lanes on market nights, standing up in the cart like a Roman charioteer. He learnt about all these works and ways, and how the land was farmed, and what was done and what was needed to be done in the farmhouses and farm-buildings, and asked the agent about all his visits of inspection and enquiry, till he felt that he knew every field and footpath on the Llantrisant estate, and could find his way to every farm-house and cottage chimney corner from the mountain to the sea. It was the absorbing interest and the great happiness of his life; and he was proud to think of all he had done for the land and for the people on it. They were excellent people, farmers, but apt to be too conservative, too much given to stick in the old ruts that their fathers and grandfathers had made, obstinately loyal to old methods in a new world. For example, there was Williams, Penyrhaul, who almost refused to grow roots, and Evan Thomas, Glascoed, who didn't believe in drainpipes, and tried to convince Vaughan that bush drainage was better for the land, and half a dozen, at least, who were sure that all artificials exhausted the soil, and the silly fellow who had brought his black Castle Martins with him from Pembrokeshire, and turned up his nose at Shorthorns and Herefords. Still, Vaughan had a way with him, and made most of them see reason sooner or later; and they all knew that there was not another estate in England or Wales that was so ready to meet its tenants half-way, and do repairs and build new barns and cowsheds very often before they were asked. Teilo Morgan gave his agent all the credit he deserved, but at the same time he could not help feeling that in spite of his disabilities, of the weakness that kept him a prisoner to these four or five rooms, so that he had not once gone over the rest of the Abbey since his return to it; in spite of his invalid and stricken days, a great deal was owing to himself and to the fresh ideas that he had brought to the management of the estate. He took in the farming journals, and was thoroughly well read in the latest literature that dealt with the various branches of agriculture, and he knew in consequence that he was well in advance of his time, in advance even of the most forward agriculturalists of the day. There were methods and schemes and ideas in full course of practical and successful working on the Liantrisant property that were absolutely unheard of on any other estate in the country. He had wanted to discuss some of these ideas in the Press; but Vaughan had dissuaded him; he said that for the present the force of prejudice was too strong. Vaughan was possibly right; all the same Teilo Morgan knew that he was making agricultural history. In the meantime, he was jotting down careful and elaborate notes on the experiments that were being tried, and in a year or two he intended to put a book on the stocks: *The Llantrisant Estates: a New Era in Farming.*

He was pondering happily in this strain; when, in a flash, a brilliant, a dazzling notion came to him. He drew a long breath of delighted wonder; then rang his hand-bell, and told the man that he might now put in the third cushion—'and give me my writing things.' A handy contraption, with paper, ink and the rest was adjusted before him, and as soon as the servant was gone, Teilo began a letter, his eyes bright with excitement.

The Tree of Life

DEAR VAUGHAN.

I know you think I'm inclined to be rather too experimental in my farming; I believe that this time you will agree that I have hit on a great idea. Don't say a word to anybody about it. I am astonished that it hasn't been thought of long ago, and my only fear is that we may be forestalled. I suppose the fact is that it has been staring us all in the face so long that we haven't noticed it!

My idea is simply this; a plantation, or orchard, if you like, of the Arbor Vitæ; and I know the exact place for it. You have often told me how Jenkins of the Garth insists on having those fields of his by the Soar down in potatoes, a most unsuitable place for such a crop. I want you to go and see him as soon as you have time, and tell him we want the use of the fields—about five acres, if I remember. Of course, he must be compensated, and, within reason, you can be as liberal as you like. I have understood from you that the soil is a deep, rich loam, in very good heart; it should be an ideal position for the culture I intend. I believe that the Arbor Vitæ will flourish anywhere, and is practically indifferent to climatic conditions: 'makes its own climate,' as one writer rather poetically expresses it. Still, its culture in this county is an experiment; and I am sure Mharadwys—I think that's the old name of those fields by the Soar—is the very spot.

The land must be thoroughly trenched. Get this put in hand as soon as you can possibly manage it. Let them leave it in ridges, so that the winter frosts can break it up. Then, if we give it a good dressing of superphosphate of lime and bone meal in the spring, and plough in September, everything will be ready for the autumn planting. You know I always insist on shallow planting; don't bury the roots in a hole; spread them out evenly within five or six inches of the surface; let them feel the sun. And when it comes to staking; mind that each tree has two stakes, crossed at the top, with the points driven into the ground at a good distance from the roots. I am sure that the single stake, close to the tree stem, with its point driven through the roots is very bad practice.

Of course, you will appreciate the importance of this new culture. The twelve distinct kinds of fruit produced by this extraordinary tree, all of them of delicious flavour, render it absolutely unique. Whatever the cost of the experiment may be, I am sure it will be made good in a very short time. And it must be remembered that while the name, *Tous les mois*, given to a kind of strawberry cultivated on the continent, really only implies that the plants fruit all through the summer and early autumn, in the case of the Arbor Vitæ, the claim may be made with literal truth. As the old writers say: 'The Arbor yielded her fruit every month.' No other cropper, however heavy, can be compared with it. And in addition to all this, the leaves are said to possess the most valuable therapeutic qualities.

Don't you agree with me that this will prove by far the most important and far-reaching of all our experiments?

I remain,

Yours sincerely,

TEILO MORGAN.

P.S. On consideration; I think it might be better to keep the dressing of super and bone meal till the autumn, just before ploughing.

And you might as well begin to look up the Nurserymen's Catalogues. As we shall be giving a large order, you may have to place it with two or three firms. I think you will find the Arbor Vitæ listed with the Coniferæ.

III

Long years after all this, two elderly men were talking together in a club smoking-room. They had the place almost to themselves; most of the members, having lunched and taken their coffee and cigarettes, had strolled away. There was a small knot of men with their heads close together over the table, chuckling and relating and hearing juicy gossip. Two or three others were dotted about the solemn, funebrous room, each apart with his paper, deep in his arm-chair. Our two were in a retired corner, which might have been called snug in any other place. They were old friends, it appeared, and one, the less elderly, had returned not long before from some far place, after an absence of many years.

'I haven't seen anything of Harry Morgan since I've been home,' he remarked. ' I suppose he's still in town.'

'Still in Beresford Street. But he doesn't get out so much now. He's getting a bit stiff in the joints. A good ten years older than I am.'

'I should like to see him again. I always thought him a very good fellow.'

'A first-rate fellow. You know that story about Bartle Frere? Man was sent to meet him at the station, and asked how he should know him. They told him to look out for an old gentleman with grey whiskers helping somebody—and he found Frere helping an old woman with a big basket out of a third-class carriage. Harry Morgan was like that—except for the whiskers.'

There was a pause; and then the man who had retold the old Sir Bartle Frere story began again.

'I don't suppose you ever heard the kindest thing Morgan ever did—one of the kindest things I've ever heard of. You know I come from his part of the country: my people used to have Plas Henoc, only a few miles from Llantrisant Abbey, the Morgans' Place. My father told me all about it; Harry kept the thing very dark. Upon my word! What is it about a man not letting his left hand know what his right is about? Morgan has lived up to that if any man ever did. Well, it was like this:

'Have you ever heard of old Teilo Morgan? He was a bit before our day. Not an old man, by the way; I don't suppose he was much over forty when he died. Well, he went the pace in the old style. He was very well known in town, not in society, or rather in damned bad society, and not far from here either. They had a picture of him in some low print of the time, with those long whiskers that used to be worn then. They didn't give his name; just called it, "The Hero of the Haymarket". You wouldn't believe it, would you, but in those days the Haymarket was the great place for night-houses—Kate Hamilton and all that lot. Morgan was in the thick of it all; but that picture annoyed him; he had those whiskers of his cut off at Truefitt's the very next day. He was the sort of man they got the silver dinner service out for, when he entertained his friends at Cremorne. And "Judge and Jury", and the *poses plastiques*, and that place in Windmill Street where they fought without the gloves—and all the rest of it.

'And it was just as bad down in the country. He used to take his London friends, male and female, down there, and lead the sort of life he lived in town, as near as he could make it. They used to tell a story, true very likely, of how he and half a dozen rapscallions like himself were putting away the port after dinner, and making a devil of a noise, all talking and shouting and cursing at the top of their voices, when Teilo seemed to pull himself together and get very grave all in a minute. "Silence gentlemen!" he called out. The rest of them took no notice; one of them started a blackguard song, and the others got ready to join in the chorus. "Hold your damned tongues, damn you!" Morgan bawled at them, and smashed a big decanter on the table. "D'you think," he said, "that that's the sort of thing for youngsters to listen to? Have you no sense of decency? Didn't I tell you that the children were coming down to dessert?" With that, he rang a bell that was by him on the table and—so the story goes—six young fellows and six girls came trooping down the big staircase: without a single stitch on them, calling out in squeaky voices: "Oh, dear Papa, what have you done to dear Mamma?" And the rest of it.'

The phrase was evidently an inclusive, vague, but altogether damnatory clause with this teller of old tales.

'Well,' he continued, 'you can imagine what the county thought of all that sort of thing. Teilo Morgan made

144

Llantrisant Abbey stink in their nostrils. Naturally, none of them would go near the place. The women, who were, perhaps, rather more particular about such matters than they are now, simply wouldn't have Morgan's name mentioned in their presence. The Duke cut him dead in the street. His subscription to the Hunt was returned. I don't think he cared. You know Garden Parties were beginning to get fashionable then, and they say Morgan sent out engraved invitation cards, with a picture of a Nymph and a Satyr on them that some artist fellow had done for him—not a nice picture at all according to county standards. And what d'ye think he had at the bottom of the card instead of R.S.V.P.?—"No clothes by request." He was a damned impudent fellow, if you like. I believe the party came off all right, with more friends from town, and most unusual games and sports on the lawn and in the shrubberies. It was said that Treowen, the Duke's son, was there; but he always swore through thick and thin that it was a lie. But it was brought up against him afterwards when he stood with Herbert for the county.

'And what d'ye think happened next? A most extraordinary thing. Nobody was prepared for it. Everyone said he would just drink and devil and wench himself to death, and a damned good riddance. Well, I'll tell you. There was one thing, you know, that everybody had to confess: in his very worst days Teilo Morgan always left the country girls alone. Never interfered with the farmers' daughters or cottage girls or anything in that way. And then, one fine day when he was up with a keeper looking after a few head of grouse he had on the mountain, what should he do but fall in love with a girl of fifteen, who lived with her mother or grandmother, I don't know which, in a cottage right up there. Mary Trevor, I believe her name was. My father had seen her once or twice afterwards driving with Morgan in his tandem: he said she was a most beautiful creature, a perfectly lovely woman. She was a type that you see sometimes in Wales: very dark, black eyes, black hair, oval face, skin a pale olive—not at all unlike those girls that used to prance up and down Arles in Southern France, with their hair done up in velvet ribbons; I don't know whether you've ever been there? There's something Oriental about that style of beauty; it doesn't last long.

'Anyhow, Teilo Morgan fell flat on the spot. He went straight down to the Abbey and packed the whole company back to town—told them they could go to hell, or bloody Jerusalem, or the Haymarket, for all he cared. As soon as they'd all gone, he was off to the mountain again. He wasn't seen at the Abbey for weeks. I am sure I don't know why he didn't marry the girl straight away; nobody knew. She said that he did marry her; but we shall come to that presently. In due course, the baby came along, and Morgan wanted to pension off the old lady and take the mother and child down to Liantrisant. But the doctors advised against it. I believe Morgan got some very good men down, and they were all inclined to shake their heads over the child. I don't think they committed

146

themselves or named any distinct disease or anything of that kind; but they were all agreed that there was a certain delicacy of constitution, and that the boy would have a much better chance if they kept him up in the mountain air for the first few years of his life. Llantrisant Abbey, I should tell you, is right down in the valley by the river, with woods and hills all round it; fine place, but rather damp and relaxing, I daresay. So, the long and short of it was that young Teilo stayed up with his mother and the old woman, and old Teilo used to come and see them for weekends, as they say now, till the boy was four or five years old; and then the old lady was looked after somewhere or other, and the mother and son went to live at the Abbey.

'Everything went on all right—except that the county people kept away—for three or four years. The child seemed well and strong, and the tutor they got in for him said he was a tremendous fellow with his books, well in advance of his age, unusually interested in his work and all that. Then he got ill, very ill indeed. I don't know what it was; some brain trouble, I should think, meningitis or something of that sort. It was touch and go for weeks, and it left the unfortunate little chap an absolute wreck at the end of it. For a long time they thought he was para-lysed; all the strength had gone out of his limbs. And the worst of it was, the mind was affected. He seemed bright enough, mind you; nothing dull or heavy about him; and I'm told you might listen to him chattering away for half an hour on end, and go away thinking he was a perfect phenomenon of a child for intelligence. But if you listened long enough, you'd hear something that would pull you up with a jerk. Crazy?—yes, and worse than crazy—mixed up in a way with a kind of sense, so that you might begin to wonder which was queer, yourself or the boy. It was a dreadful grief to the parents, especially to his father. He used to talk about his sins finding him out. I don't know, there may have been something in that. "Whips to scourge us"—perhaps so.

'They got the tutor back after some time; the child begged so hard for him that they were afraid he'd worry himself into another brain fever if they didn't give way. So he came along with instructions to make the lessons as much a farce as he liked, and the more the better; not on any account to press the boy over his work. And from what my father told me, young Teilo nearly drove the poor man off his head. He was far sharper in a way than he'd ever been before, with a memory like Macaulay's— once read, never forgotten—and an amazing appetite for learning. But then the twist in the brain would come out. Mathematics brilliant; and at the end of the lesson he'd frighten that tutor of his with a new theory of figures, some notion of the figures that we don't know of; the numbers that are between the others, something rather more than one and less than two, and so forth. It was the same with everything: there was the Secret Conquest of England a hundred years ago, that nobody was allowed to mention, and the squares that were always changing their shape in geometry, and the great continent that was hidden because Africa was on top of it, so that you couldn't see it. Then, when it came to the classics, there were fresh cases for the nouns and new moods for the verbs: and all the rest of it. Most extraordinary, and very sad for his father and mother. The poor little fellow took a tremendous interest in the family history and in the property; but I believe he hashed all that up in some infernal way. Well; it seemed there was nothing to be done.

'Then his father died. Of course, the question of the succession came up at once. Poor Mrs Morgan, as she called herself to the last, swore she was married to Teilo, but she couldn't produce any papers—any papers that were evidence of a legal marriage anyhow. I fancy the truth was that they were married in some forgotten little chapel up in the mountains by a hedge preacher or somebody of that kind, who didn't know enough to get in the registrar. Of course, Teilo ought to have known better, but probably he didn't bother at the time so long as he satisfied the girl. He may have meant to make it all right eventually, and left it too late: I don't know. Anyhow, Payne Llewellyn, the family solicitor, gave the poor woman to understand that she and the boy would have to leave Llantrisant Abbey, and off they went. They had one room in a miserable back street in Islington or Barnsbury or some such God-forsaken place and she earned a bare living in a sweater's workshop.

'Meanwhile, the property had passed to a cousin; Harry Morgan. And he hadn't been heard of; or barely

heard of; for some years. He had gone off exploring
Central Asia or the sources of the Amazon when Teilo
Morgan was in his glory—if you can put it that way. He
hadn't heard a word of Teilo's reformation or of Mary
Trevor and her boy; and when old Llewellyn was able to
get at him after considerable difficulty and delay, he never
mentioned the woman or her son. When Morgan did
come home at last, he found he didn't fancy the old
family place; called it a dismal hole, I believe. Anyhow, he
let it on a longish lease to a mental specialist—mad
doctors, they called them then—and he turned the Abbey
into a lunatic asylum.

'Then somebody told Harry about Mary Trevor, and
the poor child, and the marriage or no-marriage. He was
furious with Llewellyn. He had a search made, and when
he found them, it was just too late so far as Mary Trevor
was concerned. She had died, of grief and hard work and
semi-starvation, no doubt. But Harry took the boy away,
and finding how he was longing to go back to the
Abbey—he was quite convinced, you see, that he was the
owner of it and of all the Morgan estates—Harry got the
doctor who was running the place to take Teilo as a
patient. He was given a set of rooms to himself in a wing,
right away from the other patients. Everything was done
to encourage him in his notion that he was Teilo Morgan
of Liantrisant Abbey. Going back to the old place had
stirred up all his enthusiasm for the family, and the
property, and the management of the estates, and it
became the great interest of his life. He quite thought he

was making it the best-managed estate in the county: inaugurating a new era in English farming, and all the rest of it. Harry Morgan instructed Captain Vaughan, the Estate Agent, to see Teilo once a week, and enter into all his schemes and pretend to carry them out, and I believe Vaughan played up extremely well, though he sometimes found it difficult to keep a straight face. You see, that twist in the brain wasn't getting any better, and when it went to work on practical farming it produced some amazing results. Vaughan would be told to get this bit of land ready for pineapples, and somewhere else they were to grow olives; and what about zebras for haulage? But it kept him happy to the last. D'you know, the very day he died, he wrote a long letter of instructions to Vaughan. What d'you think it was about? You won't guess. He told Vaughan to plant the Tree of Life in a potato patch by the Soar, and gave full cultural directions.'

'God bless me ! You don't say so?'

The Major, who had listened to the long story, ruminated awhile. He had been brought up in an old-fashioned Evangelical household, and had always loved 'Revelations.' The text burned and glowed into his memory, and he said in a strong voice:

' "In the midst of the street of it, and on either side of the river, was there the tree of life, which bare twelve manner of fruits, and yielded her fruit every month: and the leaves of the tree were for the healing of the nations." '

There was only one man besides our two friends left in the darkening room; and he had fallen fast asleep in his arm-chair, with his paper on the ground before him. The Major's clear intonation woke him with a crash, and when he heard the words that were being uttered, he was seized with unspeakable and panic terror, and ran out of the room, howling (more or less) for the Committee.

But the Major having ended his text, said:

'I always thought Harry Morgan was a good fellow. But I didn't know he was such a thundering good fellow as that.'

And that was his Amen.

Out of the Picture

I

IN THE OLD days—which means anything from ten to thirty years ago—there was a question which used to be asked now and then at studio parties and Chelsea pubs. The question was:

'But who was the twisted man?'

And it was often followed by another:

'But where did M'Calmont take himself off to?'

Neither interrogation ever got an answer; save that to the second query, a young man in very full dark green corduroy trousers is reported to have said once on a time:

'Somebody told me he had been seen in Quito.'

But to this neither credit or attention was given. And it is probable from what follows that the double enigma is to be reckoned with that question as to what song the Sirens sang; if, indeed, it is not past all solution.

Going back, then, to those old days aforesaid, and rather to the earlier portion of them, when, as a journalist, I saw many strange things and people; I was once sent to view an exhibition of pictures at the Molyneux Galleries in Danby Place. Perhaps the event may be sufficiently dated by saying that the Exhibition was opened somewhere between the Battle of Sidney Street and the Coronation of King George V; and I have a feeling that it was a misty May morning when I went to see it. It was not a large exhibition: all the pictures were contained in two sizeable rooms, and as soon as I got into them I saw at once that I could make nothing of it—that is, from any serious standpoint. I cared nothing; my point of view in that instance, as in all others like it, was, that if the paper chose to send an outsider and an ignoramus to criticise works of art—especially the works of a new and tentative and experimental school—then, on the head of the paper let the just doom fall. And the school represented on this particular occasion at the Molyneux Galleries evidently represented a fierce revolt against the traditions and conventions of the elders. To begin with; my eye was caught by 'The Old Harbour.' There were buildings in vertical perspective, their walls appearing to incline together and to aspire to meet in the upper part of the canvas, and with a sense about them as if the whole mass were unstable, impermanent, void of true solidity and settlement on the earth. A mystic once told me that after he had finished his meditation and gone out into the street, he had seen the grey bulk of the houses opposite suddenly melt, evaporate, go up like smoke, leaving void nothingness in their place. And so the painter with his art had made these warehouses and Customs buildings, or whatever they were, in such a fashion that they seemed as if they also were on the very point to turn to mist, to float into the air, and to disappear. And then, for the rest, there was grey water, and segments, and portions, and particles of keels, sails, masts, ropes, decks, and deck furniture, not cohering, or fitting together, but dispersed and apart. Here, I could see, was choice matter on which the expert and art critic could exercise their knowledge and judgement. As I had neither, I made an experiment or two, and was able to inform the readers of the paper that if you walked briskly past the picture, winking both eyes as fast as possible, you really got a sort of impression of movement and activity, of ships and boats coming into harbour and sailing out of it, of sails lowered and hoisted, of an uncertain background, now obscured, now left visible as a ship in full sail passed before it. It struck me that, in my hands, art criticism was in a fair way to become a popular sport.

And then there was another picture that both attracted and distracted me. It was a big canvas, and the subject was a number of geometrical figures of all kinds, most ingeniously fitted into one another, and rainbow painted, no doubt on some occult principal of contrast and compliment and correspondence. It was called 'King Solomon's Cargoes.' I murmured: 'Gold and silver and ivory and apes and peacocks,' and looked for them. I could not see any of them, and I thought I would go back to Fleet Street, relying on my impressions of 'The Old Harbour,' which would just fill the 'two sticks' that had been allotted to the story. It was, decidedly, a case of least said, soonest mended. In spite of the defence which, as I have mentioned, I had ready; I felt I was on unsafe and treacherous ground. Who was I to sit in judgement on the work of painters? No doubt, I might say that I had looked for apes and peacocks in that picture and had found none; and, likely enough, that remark might merely serve to display my utter ignorance of the subject I was pretending to treat. But it was not written that I should escape 'King Solomon's Cargoes' so easily.

It was some years after the exhibition at the Molyneux Galleries that I found myself in a various company one evening. I saw a few people that I knew, and was talking to one of them, when the friend who had brought me along came and said:

'Do you mind if I introduce you to a man? It's M'Calmont, the painter, who says he's been wanting to meet you for years. Some criticism of yours that he read seems to have made a great impression on him.'

He took me up to a dark, slight man with a black moustache, and left me. M'Calmont made room on the settee, and began at once:

'I've been wanting to thank you for a long time for that notice you wrote in your paper about the Exhibition in the Molyneux Galleries. You'll remember? It was in Coronation year.'

I told him I thought I did remember something about it. But I wondered, internally, what sort of thanks I was going to get from a painter for my vain ribaldry. He went on:

Out of the Picture

'I said to myself at the time: "This A.M., whoever he may be, has got an eye to detect the falsities and fallacies, and I'd like to have a talk with him." Then somebody told me your name, but I left town soon after, and this is the first chance I've had.'

And, finally, it came to this: that the falsities and fallacies were the picture of 'The Old Harbour,' by Frank Guildford, and M'Calmont had enjoyed the way I had stuck my knife into the fellow.

I explained. I said I knew nothing about painting, and had been afraid that I had been guilty of ill-placed and unmannerly humour. He wouldn't hear of this.

'It was just instinct, pure instinct. You may not have the technical knowledge, but you know a silly man when you see him.'

I asked what had become of this unhappy man.

'He's what they call a fashionable painter, and makes his eight thousand a year by painting grocers and their wives—damn him!'

And he went on:

'I don't know whether you happened to see a thing I had in that Exhibition? I called it 'King Solomon's Cargoes."

I lied. I dwelt again and more forcibly on the utter unscrupulousness of my character when simulating an art critic. I said I had not seen his canvas. I had just dashed into the galleries, invented my silly game with the ships in the harbour, and run out again as soon as I had got material for my two or three paragraphs. But, in fact, I

157

remembered those purple squares, scarlet triangles, sky-blue circles very well.

M'Calmont nodded his head gloomily.

'I'm glad it didn't catch your eye. You might have had something to say to me too. You'd have been right, and you'd have been wrong. I was never a faker like Guildford. I never pretended that if you painted a bit of mast here and a scrap of a sail there and a deck in another part of the canvas you could call it painting a ship. But I did believe in abstract painting—and I do still in a way.'

I asked him to tell me all about it.

'I'd like to explain what I was after in those days. You say you know nothing about the technical side of painting. You won't want to know anything about it: it's not a technical question. It's behind all that and beyond it. But you can't talk sense in the middle of all these havers. Come away.'

I followed him out, and by devious and obscure ways he led me to an obscure tavern, where we sat down together in a quiet corner of a bulging and old-fashioned bar. They spoke his language there, since his order for 'two wee halfyins' was fulfilled without comment. But I looked at the stuff in my glass, and remembered how the poet had said that the half is greater than the whole—'greater,' I corrected mentally, 'than the double.' I added water.

'Don't kill good drink,' M'Calmont said reproachfully. '*Scelus est jugulare Falernum*, and this is better. It's the genuine Lagavulin, not the trash they sell in London for whiskey. But you were asking about abstract painting. It will be necessary to go back and away a little if we're to see what we're after. They say distance lends enchantment to the view; I'd put it myself, "lends vision," *theoria*. It may turn out, of course, that when you do see, you see enchantment, but that is just secondary; a kind of by-product, you might say, of the proposition. I'll ask you, then, if you know anything about the Kabbala of the Hebrews?'

Whatever I knew of that matter, I dissembled. I am a lover of the rich improbabilities, and I would not check this rare manifestation of them.

'Well, I don't want you to feel like a cow in a fremd loaming; so we won't go too deeply into those dark mysteries. But the Kabbalists tell us that at the Fall of Man, the Serpent did not ascend to Kether in the Tree of Life. It stopped at Daath. And that's their way of saying that the nature of man was not entirely corrupted. The Serpent poisoned and infected the logical understanding, but there was a pure, spiritual region above that which remained untouched.

'Very good. You see that? And there you have the reason why a man that's sunk deep in the blackest mud of materialism may very possibly be overcome with delight at the Fugues of Bach. You'll see how that may be? That's absolute music. It has nothing to do with Daath, the logical understanding. I'm speaking, you understand, of the pattern of sounds that reaches the ears of the hearer; just the ordered noise that he hears, if you like to put it that way. In the making of the music, no doubt, in the technical part of the creation, the understanding had its share, as the slave of the spirit. If you want to build Jerusalem with its Temple you must have your hewers of wood and stone and drawers of water. You're a writer yourself, and you know you can't do much in that way without calling in the aid of the pen-makers and the ink manufacturers and paper merchants; but you don't allow them to teach you how to turn the phrase.

'But the way the thing is fashioned is nothing to do with us. What we're concerned with is the thing we hear; and with that thing the logical understanding has just no concern at all. You'll note there's no tongue or language in which we can speak of it. There's no answer to the question: 'But what does it mean?' when that question is asked of pure music. Bach, you may say, had the gift of tongues; but in his case there's no legitimate gift of the interpretation of tongues. It's impossible to translate the language of Kether into the speech of Daath. I remember well going to hear *Lohengrin*, and there was a manner of commentary attached to the bill of the opera. I just glanced at it and saw that when the overture began I was to picture to myself a blue sky, and then to watch the wee white clouds forming on it. There you have your music critic calling in nature, and I saw in the paper, there was another of them puzzling his head over Berlioz, and decided that he was a 'pictural,' not a 'linear' composer—calling in the terms of another art. And you'll hear often enough of the 'magnificent colour' of this or that passage of music. And I don't say they can do better. But it proves what I am telling you: that the understanding has nothing to do with absolute music, and nothing to say to it.

'Aye, and what about painting? That's the question I asked myself years ago. You know Aristotle says that all art is imitation. It's a very questionable pronouncement. If I'm not mistaken he had the drama chiefly in his mind when he made it. But the drama is just an impure or mixed development of the dance. In its primitive, original form, the dance was not an imitation of anything. It was, like music, an expression of something; but that's different. You may say that the drama of the Greeks was the dance set to words. And then, there's architecture. You can't say that the Parthenon is an imitation of anything, or that Rheims Cathedral is an imitation of anything. And literature. I shan't need to tell you that all the things we value most in the finest literature are just the things that soar above the sense—that is the logical understanding of it. If you turn to the Book and read Second Samuel, one, seventeen, you'll find a statement to the effect that David lamented the decease of Saul and Jonathan; but you'll not tell me that the vital interest and value of that proposition is to be discovered in the logical sense of it. And if you read Coleridge's *Kubla Khan*, I think you'll be puzzled to find out the logical sense in it and to tell me what it is. But there you have literature almost becoming music.

'And now you see what I've been getting at all the while.'

I did not; but I forbore to say so.

'It was just this: that I asked myself why should there not be abstract or absolute painting, as well as absolute music and architecture? In the past, painting has been almost entirely Aristotelian, imitative. Why should it continue wholly on those lines? And you'll have gathered that I don't consider you solve the problem by cracking an object up into bits and scraps and pieces, and then painting the bits as they lie abroad. And if you paint a man's hands three times their natural size and draw a jackass with five legs, I'm not thinking you're any nearer to a solution. And that's how I came to paint the picture that I sent into those Galleries, that I'm glad now you didn't see. I was on the wrong track.'

He lapsed at last into silence. I broke it by making a proposition remote from pure aesthetics. He declined to accede to it.

'No, no,' said M'Calmont, 'I'll not hear of it. In the 'Crown and Thistle,' I'm in Scotland, and you're my guest. Where's the Macfarlane creature?'

When we parted soon after, he wrote his address on a scrap of paper torn from his note-book, and begged me to come and see him some evening.

'I'd like to show you the new track I've found,' he said, and vanished into the night, as we came out together.

II

It may be as well to make it clear at once that I am not the man to be daunted by the unusual. I have seen too much of it for that. I know that there are quarters, and very influential quarters, in which it is considered improper to mention such things. Every age has its conventions of propriety and impropriety: every age and every race. The missionary's wife in Africa shocked her two black servants horribly and unspeakably when she said that she was afraid the fruit was too green for a tart. Her husband's name was Green, and every (black) body knows that for a wife to utter her husband's name is both impious and obscene in the highest degree. We talk quite freely in the drawing-room in a style that would have made Dickens run out of the smoking-room, and when we write books we set down boldly words that were only forced out of the policeman of yesterday by the strict order of the Bench. It is all a matter of convention and taboo, and perhaps it is idle to ask for reasons. Mrs Green, I daresay, couldn't understand why on earth she shouldn't utter the word 'green'; and I suppose I am in much the same case when I say that I have no notion why I shouldn't mention the unusual, the odd, the extraordinary when I come across it. At any rate, I propose to defy this particular convention, here and elsewhere and always. As I was saying, I have seen too much of it to affect disbelief in its existence. I heard from the brassfounders of Clerkenwell

about a former member of their craft who had confuted
Darwin by the Hebrew alphabet and by the stars, and had
buried the pot of gold in a field, where it was found by
the navvies who were making the cutting for the Midland
Railway. I have discussed with a solicitor, in his London
office, the affairs of the J.H.V.S. Syndicate, who were
seeking for the Ark of the Covenant from the directions
of a cypher contained in that chapter of the Prophet
Ezekiel which is called Mercabah. I know all about
Campo Tosto, of Burnt Green, near Reigate, who
defended his treasures with the bow and arrow. Why,
then, should I hush up M'Calmont the painter, who drew
his artistic principles from the Hebrew Kabbala?

As a matter of fact, I thought him an interesting man,
and determined that I would see more of him. And so,
one windy night in October, a few weeks after our meeting, I set out from somewhere in the west and made up
the Gray's Inn Road. I am not certain by which street I
turned from it. I think, but I am not sure, that it was by
Acton Street. I know that I had gone too far north, and
that when I came to the bottom of the street, and trav-
ersed the King's Cross Road, I found out my mistake, and
had to incline somewhat to the right in climbing the hill.
It is a district both devious and obscure, and I suppose
that its twisting streets and unexpected squares of dusty
trees will all come to ruin before they are intelligently
explored. I had trod these mazes before, and thought I
knew them tolerably well, but it was some years since I
had been in that region, and I found myself perplexed and

at fault, while the great wind blew the leaves of shadowy trees about my head and at my feet. At last I entered a black passage at a venture, and came down a short flight of steps into an irregular open space; on which there abutted a chapel of the Countess of Huntingdon's Connexion. I went round and about this square or triangle or trapezium, which was sparsely lit, till I found the green door in a wall to which I was directed, and rang the bell under the name M'Calmont. It was M'Calmont who opened the door and, taking hold of my arm, led me down a passage, past a house all lit up, where they were singing, and so to his studio, with trees all about it, bending and tossing and straining in the wind. Inside, there was a hanging lamp, and though it was not cold, the blaze of the fire was cheerful; and lamplight and firelight glittered on the carved and gilded frames of the pictures that hung on the walls. We sat down on a big settee at a comfortable distance from the fire; and he pressed on my attention what he called 'Eela'—which is spelt, I found, 'Islay.'

And then there was more of it. Not of the spirit of the western isle, but of art, as he expounded it. It seemed that he had been forced to modify, one might say, to abandon his earlier views.

'I found out, and I was not so long about it, that you can't have absolute painting any more than you can have absolute literature. There are people, as you know, who are trying their hands at that—by writing gibberish without grammar. And *that* won't do. And I discovered that my endeavours in the direction of pure painting wouldn't do either. The principle of it is all right; but it's not for pigments. If you would carry it out, you must turn Eastern carpet-maker. And I'll maintain that there are Persian carpets as fine as any symphony of Beethoven's. They are the very analogy in colour and form of pure music.

'As it seemed that I couldn't go forward, I went back. And there, as you'll no doubt be well aware, I was in the height of the fashion. The sculptors and painters too have been trying back for the last quarter of a century. There are men who do their best to forget all the bare elements of their art, their drawing and their perspective and all the rest of it, that they may paint as if they were five years old. Another lot are off to Borrioboolah Gha, to learn the principles of sculpture from black savages. And I've no doubt there's a weary band trying to tramp back all the way to the Stone Age to see what they can find there. It's all very interesting. I'd like it fine—if they'd not call their imitations of barbarism Modern Art. And now I shall show you where I've gone back myself, so as to be in the movement.'

He barked derisively, and turning up the lamp a little, proceeded to guide me round the studio. And I felt as helpless and as futile as I had been in the old days, when I was an art critic *pour rire*.

For I was not at all sure where he had gone back, to use his own phrase. The pictures were all landscapes, painted, I conjecture, in the manner of the eighteenth century. There seemed to me, the uninstructed, as it were a dark shadow that hung over them all. Now and again there were patches of an intense and glowing blue in M'Calmont's skies; but these were contrasted with purple cloud masses rimmed with fire, with huge white clouds blown up into the sky by gathering thunder, with cloudy walls of black streaked with coppery flame. The green of the trees and of the grass was dark and livid, and the water of the pools and streams reflected something of the threat of the skies. M'Calmont had depicted open spaces in the midst of mysterious woods, narrow valleys edged with grim rocks, paths that wound in and out by lonely lands to shattered walls on a far height, trees of strange growth hanging over a well, glades glooming with twilight and the coming storm. There was an enchantment; but the incantation was of oppression and terror. There were three things that I noticed as curious: the first was that in every picture M'Calmont had introduced fire: logs burning under a broken wall, flames breaking out of yellowish smoke in the forest clearing, a fire by the well, a fire on the far hill-side. Water, also, was represented in each canvas; well, or brook, or pool in the woods; and in every one of them there was the figure of a man, the same man, so far as I could judge. The figure was roughly dressed in the costume of an eighteenth-century country-man, in ragged clothes, with a scarlet cap on his head. He was depicted as tending the invariable fire, perhaps, or leaning on his staff, or half-hidden behind the trunk of a tree, or crouching among thorns on the border of a broken road. As I passed slowly from picture to picture, I noticed that the figure became more prominent. At first, it was barely seen in the background. Then it came forward into the middle distance, and at the end of the tour, the recently painted pictures, as M'Calmont told me, it was prominent in the foreground. In one picture he led a procession of torch-bearers into a wood as the night came on; but mostly he was alone in these desolate places that M'Calmont had made. And there was about this figure an impression of distortion. There was no specific deformity, as of hunched back or misshapen limbs; but yet a distinct sense of a form twisted and awry. And the face, where it could be clearly seen, was at once piteous and malignant, as of a stricken snake, wounded and dying.

Whatever my feelings about this odd gallery of paintings may have been, I kept it to myself. I reminded M'Calmont that I was an outsider and (perhaps exaggerating a little) that I could never be an admirer of the famous slaughterhouse, since it told no story.

'You're an awful liar,' he said with engaging directness as we sat down again, 'but let that flee stick to the wa'. I told you I was going back, like the rest, but not to the ignorance of childhood or savagery. I'm returning to a great art, and exploring its possibilities. You know that the Gothic architecture was the result of the builders, first of the dark ages and then of the middle ages, exploring the possibilities of the architecture of the Romans?'

'I have heard that theory advanced,' I said, 'but I don't know that it holds the field so decisively as you seem to think. I believe that some authorities would tell you that the gothicosity of the Gothic derives, to a great extent at least, from the East.'

'I wouldn't believe a word of that tale—not that it signifies one way or the other in the argument. But I've seen churches down on the Rhone where the Gothic seems growing out of the Classic before your very eyes. There's one such at Valence: a regular Classic pediment, and all the detail of it one would call Norman, if one saw it in England. And anyone who will cast an eye over a First Pointed capital will see in a moment that it's a Corinthian capital in disguise; especially if it's got the square abacus.'

'Very good, then,' I assented, 'let us grant your doctrine of Gothic. You're applying it to painting?'

'That is so. As I said; I'm exploring the possibilities of an old school of landscape. I don't know whether it's ever struck you; but there's no doubt that some of the painters of that age anticipated the word that came to Coleridge and Wordsworth. The eighteenth-century literature was Pope. It belonged to Daath, the region of the logical understanding. To the men of that age, the poetry of the sixteenth century and the first half of the seventeenth century was just Egyptian hieroglyphics. They could not interpret a single word of it; they'd forgotten what it meant. And, naturally, they could not dream of what was to come after them. But if you look at some of their painting: you'll see the landscapes of *Kubla Khan*—the awe, and the terror, and the hidden mysteries of earth and air, water and fire. And I just meant to find out what's beyond the turn of those paths they made.'

He paused for a moment. 'But that's not painter's talk,' he went on. 'I mean, of course, that I've taken a certain school of landscape painting as my starting-point; and I will see if I can't develop it on its own lines. I hope to draw something new out of the old.'

'You have a figure, I notice, in all your pictures.'

'You must have the human figure. Without that all your scenery would dissolve and melt away. It would be just nothing at all.'

I did not ask if it was necessary that this human figure should be abhorrent of aspect. For that, I was certain, would not be painter's talk. And soon after, I went out into the labyrinth on the hill-side. It was late, and the night had grown misty, and the sound of the streets below came faintly, with strange voices.

III

I remember being told a good many years ago in the course of a cheerful evening that the one thing fatal to an actor was intelligence.

'Or if you like it better,' said the speaker, 'I will say intellect. Or, better still, that something or other in a man that can pick a character to pieces, and analyse it, and find out why it does this, that, or the other, and relate it to the plot and the other parts in the cast; and then, continuing the process, build up by careful reasoning, the impersonation out of tones of the voice, facial expression, gesture, habit of body, and so forth.'

'But,' said a gentleman in the company, 'isn't that the way to act? I thought that was how it was done.'

'That's how I do it,' replied the lecturer. 'But I haven't any illusions. The man who depicts by that method will never be a 'feerst actor,' as the German producer called it when I was in *Old Heidelberg* with Alexander. You know the story of Irving and poor Bill Terriss. Bill was ponging away for all he was worth as Henry VIII. Irving stopped him.

' "Very good, Terriss; very good indeed. I suppose you don't understand the meaning of one single word that you have uttered?"

' "No, guv'nor," said Terriss, not in the least put out. "But it'll go all right on the night."

'That's the way to act.'

'But, excuse me,' said the man who wanted to know, 'I'm afraid I don't quite grasp your meaning. *What* is the way to act?'

'You begin by not being able to give a single reason for anything you do or for your particular style of doing it. The rest comes along by itself. And I think I will help myself to another drink ere I go to that bourne . . . I don't want to miss the twelve-forty.'

It was probable, I considered, that the old actor—a dignified Priest in *Hamlet*—was right in the main. Creative work, even such secondary creative work as the actor's, is not achieved by theories or by taking thought. A man must know the grammar of his business, whatever it is; the rest, if it is to be of the first order, must be the work of the hidden flame within. And, therefore, I had grave doubts of the validity of M'Calmont's art, when I thought of the elaboration of his theories. I remembered Claude Lantier in L'Œuvre. He made up his mind to be a stark realist, to paint bunches of carrots with sincerity. But he listened to theories, and ended by hanging himself before his symbolical picture of Paris as a nude woman, whose flesh glowed with jewels, like a Byzantine icon. It was some time before I went to see him again in that retired and secret studio. I met him in Holborn a few weeks after my visit, and he asked me in a very cheerful manner whether I was recovering from his pictures by degrees— giving his short bark of laughter. I told him that I had been allowed out for the last week.

'But,' said I, willing to continue the vein of mild face-tiousness, 'you know art without a story is no good to me. Do tell me the story of that figure in all your paintings— the figure of the twisted man.'

He stared at me blankly as if he hadn't a notion what I was talking about. Then he caught sight of an east-bound 'bus in a slowly moving press of traffic, ran for it, and shook a jocular fist at me from the top of the stair. And that was the last I saw of M'Calmont for a considerable time.

I was occupied as a matter of fact all through that winter with affairs and interests of my own. What is generally and conveniently known as psychical research has always had a strong attraction for me, in spite, or perhaps because, of the obscurities, difficulties and drawbacks of the pursuit. I must say, that the usual demand of the men of physical science does not strike me as in the least rational. This demand is, I believe, that psychical phenomena should be made to conform to the laws of the laboratory experiment. The man of science says: 'I can make hydrogen by a simple process of mixing acid and water and zinc. If you don't believe me, come along now to my laboratory, and I will make hydrogen in three or four minutes, and show you how it is done, so that you can make it yourself and blow yourself up, too, if you don't follow the directions. Or, if you like, I will make hydrogen tomorrow morning at eleven, or tomorrow night at twelve, or on Saturday by written appointment.' You confess your belief in the validity and efficacy of the hydrogen process; and your scientific friend goes on: 'Very good; but you were telling me of a woman who looked in a crystal one morning, and saw and foretold correctly certain things that happened fifty miles away four hours later. Then, find that woman and bring her along to the laboratory, and let me see and hear her doing it again, and let her explain to me how she does it.' And here, I say, physical science strikes me as profoundly irrational. A great poet cannot guarantee a masterpiece to be written on demand, under the eye of an observer, by 6.50 p.m. Shillaker, the famous bat, would never undertake to reproduce his 250 not out and no chances given, against the Patagonians. He knows that when he next meets that famous eleven, he may be out for a duck in the first over. And what painter can explain how he does it? Can Dick, Tom, and Harry go to the Master, listen to a demonstration, and come away, fully prepared to equal his immortal works? Clearly, men are capable of all sorts of performances of body and spirit which are not in the least amenable to the law of the laboratory. Let us remember the historic case of one of whom it is recorded: 'at tip-cheese, or odd and even, his hand is out.' If Master Tommy Bardell had been required to demonstrate his skill at tip-cheese then and there in Court, under the immediate eye of Mr Justice Stareleigh, he would, very likely, have made a miserable fiasco.

So I have always ruled out the scientific demand and its implied conclusion as void and vain and foolish. The real difficulties in these enquiries are to be found, partly in the exquisite skill to which the art of the conjurer is sometimes brought, partly to the rarity of the faculty of keen and clear observation, partly to inaccurate and unreliable memory, a little to the commonness of lying: but most of all to the vast and bottomless credulity of the race of men. It is not a case of a plausible tale deceiving a simpleton; it is a case of homely strangers going to an hotel in a busy seaside town, telling the managing director of the concern that they are leaving him a couple of million in their wills, and living at the hotel free of payment for eight or nine months. What is to be expected when the managing director—the type is common—devotes his talents to psychical research?

Still, with all this in my mind, I persevered; perhaps not altogether displeased at the thought that, so far as clear and final and general conclusions were concerned, the quest was a hopeless one. After all, there is something eminently human in the desire of impossible things. To seek for possibilities is rather the business of the lower animals than of man. To be more specific: it had often struck me that from the singular phenomena grouped together under the heading of *poltergeist* there might, possibly or even probably, emerge a good deal of light on the doings and showings of modern spiritualism. In both cases, naturally, a huge discount has to be made. No doubt, the *poltergeist* was often a bad child, delighting in annoying, alarming, and humbugging its elders, delighting also in playing the leading part in the comedy. Sometimes, hysteria was to be expected; and hysteria is capable of anything. But it seems to me that there was a very considerable remanent of *poltergeist* cases in which mischief and trickery and ordinary hysteria were necessarily excluded from consideration. As to the other end of the enquiry, spiritualism; its history might, in a sense, be called a sad one. The last time I looked into the leading spiritualist journal I saw on one page a description of the unpleasing methods by which the medium had hidden the flowers that were to drop later from the spirit world on to the séance table; on another page was a brief announcement that an eminent spiritualist had declared the equally eminent Mr X, the spirit photographer, to be a highly fraudulent person. For the time, at all events, I decided on occupying myself with the manifestations of the simple *poltergeist*.

And, as it happened, a favourable opportunity came in my way. Soon after my encounter with M'Calmont in Holborn, I ran across an old acquaintance of mine, Manning, who was something in the British Museum. A few years before, when he had been a lodger in a Bloomsbury street, I had been accustomed to see a good deal of him; but he had married and gone to live with his wife on some remote heights up at Hornsey, and we had not encountered one another for some time. We found a nook in which we could exchange such news as we had, and I heard a good deal about the fine old garden, 'above the London smoke,' and of great success with roses. Then came something interesting.

'Six months ago,' Manning began, 'we took a boarder. He's a boy of fifteen, and his father, Richards, an old friend of mine, has got a job in the East, which will keep him there for some years. He asked me if my wife and I would take charge of the lad for the next year or two, anyhow. The mother is dead, and, as Richards put it, he didn't want to leave his son with strangers. The young fellow is a day boy at Westminster, so we don't see too much of him, in term-time at all events.

'Well, he came along and seemed a decent young chap enough, and didn't give any trouble—till the last week or so. And now we don't know what to do about him.'

176

'What's wrong?' I asked. 'Stays out late at night and comes home drunk? That sort of thing?'

'Not a bit of it. He sticks to his work all of the evening and goes to bed soon after ten. But, wherever he is, things go smash. It began with a stone coming through the dining-room window. I thought, naturally, some hooligan had thrown it from the street, and rushed out. The only people near enough to have done it were a couple of quiet old ladies walking along and chatting to each other about the vicar. Another night the clock jumped from the shelf on to the table. Then he went into the kitchen to get me a box of matches, and the plates on the dresser began falling about. It worries my wife—and it bothers me too. Young Richards says he doesn't do it. No doubt he does, all the same; but I haven't succeeded in catching him at it, so far. I suppose I shall have to write to his father, and that won't be pleasant.'

I saw my chance. I told Manning that young Richards must be regarded, not as an infernal nuisance, but as an interesting case. On my earnest petition, Mrs Manning being, I believe, rather glad to have another man on the premises, I became the second paying guest at the Horn-sey house, promising myself important and first-hand evidence. And I had better say at once that I was disappointed. As young Richards pored over his home-work at a side table, I saw a small piece of Samian ware rise up from the table at the other end of the room, hover, or seem to hover, for an instant, and then fall to the floor, breaking into fragments. I could not see how Richards could possibly be the conscious agent in this event. There was, certainly, no apparatus of threads or wires concerned in the destruction of the Samian bowl. The boy looked frightened and furious; and I found out that he had been thrashed at his preparatory school for 'wilful destruction.' But, from the enquirer's point of view, 'what next?' It seemed that one was reduced to posit an unknown force, devoid of conscious or intelligent direction, and wholly outside and beyond the sphere of physical science. And yet; this was something.

Richards in himself was an entirely ordinary and normal boy; a very decent fellow, I should say, neither too stupid nor too intelligent. It was only in his appearance that there was something not quite ordinary. I do not know that he was short for his age, but his breadth of chest made him appear short, and gave a certain vague impression of deformity, and also of considerable strength.

I had been staying with the Mannings for six or seven weeks, and it was drawing towards the darkest and shortest days in the year. There was a succession of heavy fogs, and it was after one of these that the 'Horrible Dwarf' scare began its course in the papers. A small child, living with its parents in a back street of Westminster, had been sent on some errand to a shop round the corner. The fog was thick down there by the river, but the distance was short, the little girl went to the shop for her mother every other day, and there were no roads to be crossed. She came back crying, and evidently badly frightened, having dropped the sixpenn'orth of tea, or whatever it was.

178

Out of the Picture

When she had been soothed into coherence, she told a tale of a 'dreadful little man,' who came out of a passage, and bent down with all his teeth showing, and put out his hands as if he would take her by the throat and kill her— and then disappeared into the fog, without saying a word. Of course the neighbours came swarming to hear all about it, and deafened each other with conjectures of an impossible kind, and proposed moves and measures which led nowhere. On the whole, it was to be gathered that the horrible little man must be a stranger, since no dwarfs were known to inhabit the neighbourhood. The police were called in, and made very little of the business, ranking the offender with those tiresome but not dangerous semi-lunatics who cut off girls' hair on the bus, or slash their clothes in the street. The paragraphs in the press were brief, and some people were inclined to think that the small messenger had let the tea or sugar spill into the gutter and had invented the dwarf in order to escape punishment. But, then, in a couple of days, there was something more serious. Late on a dismal afternoon, a man who was taking a short cut through an unfrequented by-street off the Tottenham Court Road, felt, as he said, a violent punch in the back, and found himself at the bottom of a flight of area stairs. He was bruised and shaken, but conscious, and as he looked up, he saw an ugly little man grinning at him through the railings. He struggled to his feet, and ran up the steps, shouting: 'Stop thief!' There were two or three people about, who came running; but they had seen nothing. Then, on another evening, five or six days later, a girl looking into a shop window in Camden Town, became aware that there was a short man, 'with a nasty look on his face,' standing beside her, and the next moment she felt a piercing pain in her arm, screamed out in agony and fear, and fainted. There was hurry and bustle, shouting and confusion, running here and there from all quarters, but by the time the girl had come to herself and was able to say what had happened to her, the assailant had disappeared. A doctor came up and found a long needle almost buried in her arm. The newspaper paragraphs had become halfcolumns, and people began to be afraid. And the next outrage of the 'Horrible Dwarf' was again at Westminster; and close to the place where the small messenger had been frightened. Again there was a dense fog; rather a thick white mist, deadening to sound, so that in those narrow streets where there is little wheeled traffic on the brightest days, such noises as these were could hardly be heard, and seemed dull and muffled as if they came from a place far off. But through this thick, stilled silence there broke a lamentable complaint. A man, making his way homeward, cautiously, warily, and slowly, passed through one of these by-streets where, for some years, there had been a patch of wretched and wasted land. Four or five cottages had been pulled down, and for some reason or another the plans for re-building had fallen through, and the plot where the houses stood lay as the house-breakers had left it. There were cavernous remains of underground rooms or cellars, brickbat mountains, plaster valleys, all scattered over with fragments of mouldering beams and jagged with shattered slates; a very dismal and ruined place, separated from the pavement by a line of broken-down palings. As the homeward-bound man felt his way along the street, he thought he heard a noise of crying, a very faint, sad sound. He stopped and listened by a window, where the light from within was barely apparent through the thick, white folds of mist, and wondered whether the sound came from a child, shut up alone and frightened. He could not satisfy himself that this was so, and walked on a few paces, still listening, and thinking that he was drawing nearer to the noise of crying. He was now by the palings that hedged off the waste land, and he became sure that here was the scene of the trouble. He broke through the rotten fence, and went prowling and stumbling about, well aware, as he had often passed that way, that he might very well come to grief himself in the broken-down ruin and confusion of the place. But, with good fortune, he came without disaster to a wretched child lying on his back amidst the rubbish, sobbing and wailing most piteously. The man gave him a cheerful 'What's the matter, Tommy? Come along, and we'll make it all right,' and tried to lift the child to his feet. But the poor misery cried out in sharper anguish, and the man raised him as gently as he could and bore him away, dreadfully afraid all the while that he might stumble and fall and, as he said afterwards, do the poor little beggar in.

However, he brought his burden safely out of the horrible pits, and rang the bell at the first house he came to.

The Children of the Pool

The rescuer and the people of the house saw a terrible sight. It was a poor place, with a bed in the sitting-room, and on this they laid the wreckage. It was a boy of nine or ten. One leg seemed bent under him, and when they tried to straighten it the child screamed with pain. But it was the boy's face that frightened them. It was all swollen and bloody, and black with bruises, and the blood was still gushing from the nostrils, which were as if they had been stamped on by the hoof of a horse. One went out and shouted through the fog for the police; and in time the poor boy was taken in an ambulance to the hospital. In a day or two, a little mended and recovered, he told his tale of a twisted man that came out of the mist, and took him up as if he would have broken him, and carried him over the fence and threw him down, and then stamped with his feet on his face.

The newspapers altered their headline to 'Devilish Dwarf', and cursed the police—and so forth.

And it was after this most detestable outrage that Manning horrified me one night, as we sat by the fire with the rest of the house abed. He told me that he was seriously afraid that young Richards was guilty of these abominations. He urged that they had all taken place at a time when the boy was on his way from Westminster to Hornsey, that he had certainly been late home on the occasions of the first and last of the outrages. He dwelt on his dwarfish appearance, on his great strength, but above all on those abnormal activities which had interested me in the first place.

'You know yourself there's something queer about the fellow. Upon my word, I'm afraid he's the man. And if we don't do something, it will come to murder.'

I was, indeed, horrified for a moment when he began, but at the end I laughed, I am glad to remember. I told him that the fog would amply account for Richards's late return on the two occasions he had mentioned; that to the best of my recollection he had been back in good time on the other two evenings of outrage; and finally, and most conclusively, that he was talking nonsense. 'Excepting only that singular faculty or fatality of his, he's a very ordinary boy, and a good sort.'

In short, I laughed him out of it. Happily, there were no more horrors of the 'Devilish Dwarf' order for the rest of the winter. They stopped as suddenly as they had begun; and in the succeeding calm somebody found sense enough to write an article pointing out the helplessness of the police when confronted with the motiveless outrages of a maniac. The new generation heard all about the doings of Jack the Ripper, and the analogy seemed fair enough. And at the same time—it was, of course, pure coincidence—the *poltergeist* activity, or possession, or whatever it was, of young Richards dwindled and ceased. The house on the Hornsey heights was in all respects at peace with itself when I left it for the valley of London in the early spring.

IV

Extract from a letter received about eighteen months after 'the early spring' mentioned above.

. . . Now, as to this M'Calmont business. In your place, I should certainly go no farther—or 'further'—I never know which is right and which is wrong. There's no question of bringing the story to its logical conclusion, because there isn't one. Your theories and conjectures and the rest of it may be all right—and they may be all wrong. And just remember that for all we know M'Calmont may turn up any day, and that might be a nasty business for you. I remember Sandy M'Calmont very well, and he always struck me as a man who would be extremely (shall we say) tenacious, if he got in a temper.

I note what you say about your visit to his studio in the spring of last year. In the first place; as to the man himself. You say he struck you as very much changed: 'silent, morose, and apparently not in the least glad to see me.' And I gather that the Lagavulin touch was conspicuous by its absence. I don't think there's much significance in that. There are genial Scotchmen and frozen Scotchmen, and sometimes and naturally enough you have samples of both temperaments in one man. And, as I've just said, he always struck me as having a reserve of grimness. One of his race gave me a most cordial invitation to dine with him at his club, and when the evening came, I was going to say, he didn't speak half a dozen words. That's a figure of speech; but, to be strictly accurate, if he had been 'measured up,' I don't think his remarks all through the evening would have exceeded a hundred words. He was all right the next time we met. Some of them are like that.

You say that all the pictures you had seen when you went to the studio the autumn before had been cleared away, and that there was a new lot on the walls. The change you noticed is certainly interesting: the reduction of the elaborate landscapes into mere backgrounds, the trees barely indicated, the detail shadowy, and so forth: the Twisted Man promoted from a sort of super to be the real subject of the picture—'a devilish figure,' as you say, with, I gather, minor demons grouped about him, being instructed in strange traps and chases, in obscure employments, in pastimes that did not strike you as too agreeable. I was rather reminded of an old lacquer bureau I grew up with. I remember one of the drawers was decorated with a design of a golden garden of unearthly trees, in which Chinamen in golden robes tormented a porcupine with long wands of gold. All this was certainly very odd. You didn't like M'Calmont's manner when he said: 'You asked me for the story of the Twisted Man and here it is'? I don't see much in that. But that particular gesture in one of the pictures: the man pointing to an indistinct figure on the ground, and lifting up his foot above it: well . . . Still, as you can see for yourself, there's nothing you can fasten on in that. You can't charge a painter with the crimes he chooses to paint. And that's the fatal flaw in the whole of your case; if you think you have a case.

Of course I remember that awful business of the poor girl in the July following. It was one of the most hideous and revolting things that have happened in my time; and I think that we should both agree that Fleet Street, with all its faults, rendered a public service by its suppression of most of the facts. I knew Selwyn of the *Gazette*, who was put on the country end of the story. He managed to see a sort of diary the girl had kept—about her visits to London and all that. I don't care to recall what he told me. But there again, when you try to put two and two together, you'll find it can't be done. There was nothing in those papers that Selwyn looked at to connect the unfortunate wretch with the studio. As you say, that square in Bloomsbury where the body was found is not a great distance off, but that's nothing to go on.

And, after all, it seems to me that either way, you would be well advised to let it alone. The man has gone away, and it seems likely that he will stay away, so there's no fear of any recurrence of these abominations. But, on the other hand, he *may* come back, and if he did, you might find yourself in the dock on a charge of criminal libel. And I don't think that such evidence as you have is anything like strong enough for you to put up a good defence. I say again: drop it.

I took this advice, so far as making any representations to the police authorities was concerned. After some years—

nine, getting on for ten—nothing has been heard of M'Calmont. A cousin of his eventually received authority to deal with the pictures in the studio. Some of the earlier canvases appeared in due course in the dealers' shops round St James's and Bond Street, and others went to the auction rooms, and realised very fair prices. There is a movement, I have gathered, in certain circles of art criticism, to appreciate M'Calmont's work very highly. One critic wrote lately: 'It is all old school, if you like, but there is something there that the old school never had; and I don't think that any of us quite know what it is. And I am convinced that collectors, public and private, will do well to keep a very keen eye on M'Calmont. At the present prices they are undoubted bargains.'

And the studios are still asking where M'Calmont got his model for the wonderful Twisted Man.

There was one circumstance which I failed to mention, when I consulted the friend who wrote me the letter of advice. I am not sure why I left it out of my story; possibly from a whimsical dislike of making the case too complete, possibly from a feeling, equally whimsical, that it was as well to keep one card at least safe and secret in my own hand.

But, two nights after the discovery of the package in Irving Square, when horror was still black and raging, I felt that I must visit that secret studio on the hill-side. It was a clear night with a red moon, just past the full, rising out of a low band of clouds, and this time I found my way without any difficulty. And just as I came down the flight of steps that led into the open square, I saw the green door of M'Calmont's studio open; very cautiously at first, inch by inch, and then wider, and a figure, vague against the darkness behind it, seemed to peer about for a moment. Then, the door was opened wide, and as quickly shut, and I saw a man, all twisted and bent so as to be dwarf-like, go capering with fantastic and extravagant gestures across the scene of light, and vanish into a narrow passage which led down the hill between garden walls and the shadowy boughs of trees. I stood still, beaten back into the shelter of my steps, drawing a long breath. I had recognised very well that dancing and terrible figure, and I was quite overcome by the utter impossibility of that which I had certainly seen. I had been living for some time with gathering suspicions of some dreadful and mysterious connection between the work of the studio and the horror of the waste place in Westminster; but they had been vague surmises and unshapen fears. But this was delirium; nightmare walking visibly abroad. I shook myself out of my terror and went briskly up to the studio door and rang the bell.

The door was opened by M'Calmont's handy man whom I had seen pottering about on my last visit. I asked him if Mr M'Calmont were at home.

'Not at the moment, sir,' he replied. 'But please to step in. Mr M'Calmont told me he'd be back in a minute; he's only gone to post a letter—and I'm sure he'd be very sorry to miss you.'

Out of the Picture

I followed the man to the studio, which was all lit up. I stood there in a great bewilderment.

'But, William,' I said, 'I saw somebody come out by that door just as I was coming down the steps. But it was a twisted sort of man, like that man in all Mr M'Calmont's pictures. I thought it must be the model.' The notion had flashed into my mind that moment, as with a deep sigh of relief.

William looked puzzled.

'It must have been Mr M'Calmont, sir. There's nobody else been here tonight. He went out a couple of minutes ago.'

'But the man I saw was twisted; crooked. And he was dancing about like a lunatic.'

'Then, sir, I think that was Mr M'Calmont all right. I expect he was doing what he calls his Physical Jerks, thinking there would be nobody about to see him. He says it's strongly recommended by the doctors. But do be seated, sir, if you please.'

I was staring at a great sheet of paper on an easel. It was covered with black charcoal outlines, to me significant and most awful. I had heard something of the contents of the package that had been found under the bushes of Irving Square.

I told the man I really could not wait. I hurried out of the place, and struck away up to the north, and made as quickly as I could for the broad and jangling streets, and so got home at last, avoiding dark narrows and short cuts all the way.

The Children of the Pool

I do not know how long William waited for his master to return. But he waited vainly.

Change

'HERE,' said old Mr Vincent Rimmer, fumbling in the pigeon-holes of his great and ancient bureau, 'is an oddity which may interest you.'

He drew a sheet of paper out of the dark place where it had been hidden, and handed it to Reynolds, his curious guest. The oddity was an ordinary sheet of notepaper, of a sort which has long been popular; a bluish grey with slight flecks and streaks of a darker blue embedded in its substance. It had yellowed a little with age at the edges. The outer page was blank; Reynolds laid it open, and spread it out on the table beside his chair. He read something like this:

```
a aa e ee i e ee
aa i i o e ee o
ee ee i aa o oo o
a o a a e i ee
e o i ee a e i
```

Reynolds scanned it with stupefied perplexity.

'What on earth is it?' he said. 'Does it mean anything? Is it a cypher, or a silly game, or what?'

Mr Rimmer chuckled. 'I thought it might puzzle you,' he remarked. 'Do you happen to notice anything about the writing; anything out of the way at all?'

Reynolds scanned the document more closely.

'Well, I don't know that there is anything out of the way in the script itself. The letters are rather big, perhaps, and they are rather clumsily formed. But it's difficult to judge handwriting by a few letters, repeated again and again. But, apart from the writing, what is it?'

'That's a question that must wait a bit. There are many strange things related to that bit of paper. But one of the strangest things about it is this; that it is intimately connected with the Darren Mystery.'

'What Mystery did you say? The Darren Mystery? I don't think I ever heard of it.'

'Well, it was a little before your time. And, in any case, I don't see how you could have heard of it. There were, certainly, some very curious and unusual circumstances in the case, but I don't think that they were generally known, and if they were known, they were not understood. You don't wonder at that, perhaps, when you consider that the bit of paper before you was one of those circumstances.'

'But what exactly happened?'

'That is largely a matter of conjecture. But, anyhow, here's the outside of the case, for a beginning. Now, to start with, I don't suppose you've ever been to Meirion?

192

Change

Well, you should go. It's a beautiful county, in West Wales, with a fine sea-coast, and some very pleasant places to stay at, and none of them too large or too popular. One of the smallest of these places, Trenant, is just a village. There is a wooded height above it called the Allt; and down below, the church, with a Celtic cross in the churchyard, a dozen or so of cottages, a row of lodging-houses on the slope round the corner, a few more cottages dotted along the road to Meiros, and that's all. Below the village are marshy meadows where the brook that comes from the hills spreads abroad, and then the dunes, and the sea, stretching away to the Dragon's Head in the far east and enclosed to the west by the beginning of the limestone cliffs. There are fine, broad sands all the way between Trenant and Porth, the market-town, about a mile and a half away, and it's just the place for children.

'Well, just forty-five years ago, Trenant was having a very successful season. In August there must have been eighteen or nineteen visitors in the village. I was staying in Porth at the time, and, when I walked over, it struck me that the Trenant beach was quite crowded—eight or nine children castle-building and learning to swim, and looking for shells, and all the usual diversions. The grown-up people sat in groups on the edge of the dunes and read and gossiped, or took a turn towards Porth, or perhaps tried to catch prawns in the rock-pools at the other end of the sands. Altogether a very pleasant, happy scene in its simple way, and, as it was a beautiful summer, I have no doubt they all enjoyed themselves very much. I

193

walked to Trenant and back three or four times, and I noticed that most of the children were more or less in the charge of a very pretty dark girl, quite young, who seemed to advise in laying out the ground-plan of the castle, and to take off her stockings and tuck up her skirts—we thought a lot of Legs in those days—when the bathers required supervision. She also indicated the kinds of shells which deserved the attention of collectors: an extremely serviceable girl.

'It seemed that this girl, Alice Hayes, was really in charge of the children—or of the greater part of them. She was a sort of nursery-governess or lady of all work to Mrs Brown, who had come down from London in the early part of July with Miss Hayes and little Michael, a child of eight, who refused to recover nicely from his attack of measles. Mr Brown had joined them at the end of the month with the two elder children, Jack and Rosamund. Then, there were the Smiths, with their little family, and the Robinsons with their three; and the fathers and mothers, sitting on the beach every morning, got to know each other very easily. Mrs Smith and Mrs Robinson soon appreciated Miss Hayes's merits as a child-herd; they noticed that Mrs Brown sat placid and went on knitting in the sun, quite safe and unperturbed, while they suffered from recurrent alarms. Jack Smith, though barely fourteen, would be seen dashing through the waves, out to sea, as if he had quite made up his mind to swim to the Dragon's Head, about twenty miles away, or Jane Robinson, in bright pink, would appear suddenly right away among the rocks of the point, ready to vanish into the perilous unknown round the corner. Hence, alarums and excursions, tiresome expeditions of rescue and remonstrance, through soft sand or over slippery rocks under a hot sun. And then these ladies would discover that certain of their offspring had entirely disappeared or were altogether missing from the land-scape; and dreadful and true tales of children who had driven tunnels into the sand and had been overwhelmed therein rushed to the mind. And all the while Mrs Brown sat serene, confident in the overseership of her Miss Hayes. So, as it was to be gathered, the other two took counsel together. Mrs Brown was approached, and something called an arrangement was made, by which Miss Hayes undertook the joint mastership of all three packs, greatly to the ease of Mrs Smith and Mrs Robin-son.

It was about this time, I suppose, that I got to know this group of holiday-makers. I had met Smith, whom I knew slightly in town, in the streets of Porth, just as I was setting out for one of my morning walks. We strolled together to Trenant on the firm sand down by the water's edge, and introductions went round, and so I joined the party, and sat with them, watching the various diversions of the children and the capable superintendence of Miss Hayes.

'Now there's a queer thing about this little place,' said Brown, a genial man, connected, I believe, with Lloyd's. 'Wouldn't you say this was as healthy a spot as any you could find? Well sheltered from the north, southern aspect, never too cold in winter, fresh sea-breeze in summer: what could you have more?'

'Well,' I replied, 'it always agrees with me very well: a little relaxing, perhaps, but I like being relaxed. Isn't it a healthy place, then? What makes you think so?'

'I'll tell you. We have rooms in Govan Terrace, up there on the hill-side. The other night I woke up with a coughing fit. I got out of bed to get a drink of water, and then had a look out of the windows to see what sort of night it was. I didn't like the look of those clouds in the south-west after sun-set the night before. As you can see, the upper windows of Govan Terrace command a good many of the village houses. And, do you know, there was a light in almost every house? At two o'clock in the morning. Apparently the village is full of sick people. But who would have thought it?'

We were sitting a little apart from the rest. Smith had brought a London paper from Porth and he and Robinson had their heads together over the City article. The three women were knitting and talking hard, and down by the blue, creaming water Miss Hayes and her crew were playing happily in the sunshine.

'Do you mind,' I said to Brown, 'if I swear you to secrecy? A limited secrecy: I don't want you to speak of this to any of the village people. They wouldn't like it. And have you told your wife or any of the party about what you saw?'

'As a matter of fact, I haven't said a word to anybody. Illness isn't a very cheerful topic for a holiday, is it? But what's up? You don't mean to say there's some sort of epidemic in the place that they're keeping dark? I say! That would be awful. We should have to leave at once. Think of the children.'

'Nothing of the kind. I don't think that there's a single case of illness in the place—unless you count old Thomas Evans, who has been in what he calls a decline for thirty years. You won't say anything? Then I'm going to give you a shock. The people have a light burning in their houses all night to keep out the fairies.'

I must say it was a success. Brown looked frightened. Not of the fairies; most certainly not; rather at the reversion of his established order of things. He occupied his business in the City; he lived in an extremely comfortable house at Addiscombe; he was a keen though sane adherent of the Liberal Party; and in the world between these points there was no room at all either for fairies or for people who believed in fairies. The latter were almost as fabulous to him as the former, and still more objectionable.

'Look here!' he said at last. 'You're pulling my leg. Nobody believes in fairies. They haven't for hundreds of years. Shakespeare didn't believe in fairies. He says so.'

I let him run on. He implored me to tell him whether it was typhoid, or only measles, or even chicken-pox. I said at last:

'You seem very positive on the subject of fairies. Are you sure there are no such things?'

'Of course I am,' said Brown, very crossly.

'How do you know?'

It is a shocking thing to be asked a question like that, to which, be it observed, there is no answer. I left him seething dangerously.

'Remember,' I said, 'not a word of lit windows to anybody; but if you are uneasy as to epidemics, ask the doctor about it.'

He nodded his head glumly. I knew he was drawing all sorts of false conclusions; and for the rest of our stay I would say that he did not seek me out—until the last day of his visit. I had no doubt that he put me down as a believer in fairies and a maniac; but it is, I consider, good for men who live between the City and Liberal politics and Addiscombe to be made to realise that there is a world elsewhere. And, as it happens, it was quite true that most of the Trenant people believed in the fairies and were horribly afraid of them.

But this was only an interlude. I often strolled over and joined the party. And I took up my freedom with the young members by contributing posts and a tennis net to the beach sports. They had brought down rackets and balls, in the vague idea that they might be able to get a game somehow and somewhere, and my contribution was warmly welcomed. I helped Miss Hayes to fix the net, and she marked out the court, with the help of many suggestions from the elder children, to which she did not pay the slightest attention. I think the constant disputes as to whether the ball was 'in' or 'out' brightened the game, though Wimbledon would not have approved. And sometimes the elder children accompanied their parents to Porth in the evening and watched the famous Japanese Jugglers or Pepper's Ghost at the Assembly Rooms, or listened to the Mysterious Musicians at the De Barry Gardens—and altogether everybody had, you would say, a very jolly time.

It all came to a dreadful end. One morning when I had come out on my usual morning stroll from Porth, and had got to the camping ground of the party at the edge of the dunes, I found somewhat to my surprise that there was nobody there. I was afraid that Brown had been in part justified in his dread of concealed epidemics, and that some of the children had 'caught something' in the village. So I walked up in the direction of Govan Terrace, and found Brown standing at the bottom of his flight of steps, and looking very much upset.

I hailed him.

'I say,' I began, 'I hope you weren't right, after all. None of the children down with measles, or anything of that sort?'

'It's something worse than measles. We none of us know what has happened. The doctor can make nothing of it. Come in, and we can talk it over.'

Just then a procession came down the steps leading from a house a few doors further on. First of all there was the porter from the station, with a pile of luggage on his truck. Then there came the two elder Smith children, Jack and Millicent, and finally, Mr and Mrs Smith. Mr Smith was carrying something wrapped in a bundle in his arms.

'Where's Bob?' He was the youngest; a brave, rosy little man of five or six.

'Smith's carrying him,' murmured Brown.

What's happened? Has he hurt himself on the rocks? I hope it's nothing serious.'

I was going forward to make my enquiries, but Brown put a hand on my arm and checked me. Then I looked at the Smith party more closely, and I saw at once that there was something very much amiss. The two elder children had been crying, though the boy was doing his best to put up a brave face against disaster—whatever it was. Mrs Smith had drawn her veil over her face, and stumbled as she walked, and on Smith's face there was a horror as of ill dreams.

'Look,' said Brown in his low voice.

Smith had half turned, as he set out with his burden to walk down the hill to the station. I don't think he knew we were there; I don't think any of the party had noticed us as we stood on the bottom step, half-hidden by a blossoming shrub. But as he turned uncertainly, like a man in the dark, the wrappings fell away a little from what he carried, and I saw a little wizened, yellow face peering out; malignant, deplorable.

I turned helplessly to Brown, as that most wretched procession went on its way and vanished out of sight.

Change

'What on earth has happened? That's not Bobby. Who is it?'

'Come into the house,' said Brown, and he went before me up the long flight of steps that led to the terrace.

There was a shriek and a noise of thin, shrill, high-pitched laughter as we came into the lodging-house.

'That's Miss Hayes in blaspheming hysterics,' said Brown grimly. 'My wife's looking after her. The children are in the room at the back. I daren't let them go out by themselves in this awful place.' He beat with his foot on the floor and glared at me, awe-struck, a solid man shaken.

'Well,' he said at last, 'I'll tell you what we know; and as far as I can make out, that's very little. However. . . . You know Miss Hayes, who helps Mrs Brown with the children, had more or less taken over charge of the lot; the young Robinsons and the Smiths, too. You've seen how well she looks after them all on the sands in the morning. In the afternoon she's been taking them inland for a change. You know there's beautiful country if you go a little way inland; rather wild and woody; but still very nice; pleasant and shady. Miss Hayes thought that the all-day glare of the sun on the sands might not be very good for the small ones, and my wife agreed with her. So they took their teas with them and picnicked in the woods and enjoyed themselves very much, I believe. They didn't go more than a couple of miles or three at the outside; and the little ones used to take turns in a go-cart. They never seemed too tired.

201

The Children of the Pool

'Yesterday at lunch they were talking about some caves at a place called the Darren, about two miles away. My children seemed very anxious to see them, and Mrs Probert, our landlady, said they were quite safe, so the Smiths and Robinsons were called in, and they were enthusiastic, too; and the whole party set off with their tea-baskets, and candles and matches, in Miss Hayes's charge. Somehow they made a later start than usual, and from what I could make out they enjoyed themselves so much in the cool dark cave, first of all exploring, and then looking for treasure, and winding up with tea by candlelight, that they didn't notice how the time was going—nobody had a watch—and by the time they'd packed up their traps and come out from underground, it was quite dark. They had a little trouble making out the way at first, but not very much, and came along in high spirits, tumbling over molehills and each other, and finding it all quite an adventure.

'They had got down in the road there, and were sorting themselves out into the three parties, when somebody called out: 'Where's Bobby Smith?' Well, he wasn't there. The usual story; everybody thought he was with somebody else. They were all mixed up in the dark, talking and laughing and shrieking at the top of their voices, and taking everything for granted—I suppose it was like that. But poor little Bob was missing. You can guess what a scene there was. Everybody was much too frightened to scold Miss Hayes, who had no doubt been extremely careless, to say the least of it—not like her. Robinson pulled us together. He told Mrs Smith that the little chap would be perfectly all right: there were no precipices to fall over and no water to fall into, the way they'd been, that it was a warm night, and the child had had a good stuffing tea, and he would be as right as rain when they found him. So we got a man from the farm, with a lantern, and Miss Hayes to show us exactly where they'd been, and Smith and Robinson and I went off to find poor Bobby, feeling a good deal better than at first. I noticed that the farm man seemed a good deal put out when we told him what had happened and where we were going. 'Got lost in the Darren,' he said, 'indeed, that is a pity.' That set Smith off at once; and he asked Williams what he meant; what was the matter with the place? Williams said there was nothing the matter with it at all whatever but it was 'a tiresome place to be in after dark'. That reminded me of what you were saying a couple of weeks ago about the people here. 'Some damned superstitious nonsense,' I said to myself, and thanked God it was nothing worse. I thought the fellow might be going to tell us of a masked bog or something like that. I gave Smith a hint in a whisper as to where the land lay; and we went on, hoping to come on little Bob any minute. Nearly all the way we were going through open fields without any cover or bracken or anything of that sort, and Williams kept twirling his lantern, and Miss Hayes and the rest of us called out the child's name; there didn't seem much chance of missing him.

'However, we saw nothing of him—till we got to the Darren. It's an odd sort of place, I should think. You're in an ordinary field, with a gentle upward slope, and you come to a gate, and down you go into a deep, narrow valley; a regular nest of valleys as far as I could make out in the dark, one leading into another, and the sides covered with trees. The famous caves were on one of these steep slopes, and, of course, we all went in. They didn't stretch far; nobody could have got lost in them, even if the candles gave out. We searched the place thoroughly, and saw where the children had had their tea: no signs of Bobby. So we went on down the valley between the woods, till we came to where it opens out into a wide space, with one tree growing all alone in the middle. And then we heard a miserable whining noise, like some little creature that's got hurt. And there under the tree was— what you saw poor Smith carrying in his arms this morning.

'It fought like a wild cat when Smith tried to pick it up, and jabbered some unearthly sort of gibberish. The Miss Hayes came along and seemed to soothe it; and it's been quiet ever since. The man with the lantern was shaking with terror; the sweat was pouring down his face.'

I stared hard at Brown. 'And,' I thought to myself, 'you are very much in the same condition as Williams.' Brown was obviously overcome with dread.

We sat there in silence.

'Why do you say 'it'?' I asked. Why don't you say 'him'?'

'You saw.'

Do you mean to tell me seriously that you don't believe that child you helped to bring home was Bobby? What does Mrs Smith say?'

'She says the clothes are the same. I suppose it must be Bobby. The doctor from Porth says the child must have had a severe shock. I don't think he knows anything about it.'

He stuttered over his words, and said at last:

'I was thinking of what you said about the lighted windows. I hoped you might be able to help. Can you do anything?

We are leaving this afternoon; all of us. Is there nothing to be done?'

'I'm afraid not.'

I had nothing else to say. We shook hands and parted without more words.

The next day I walked over to the Darren. There was something fearful about the place, even in the haze of a golden afternoon. As Brown had said, the entrance and the disclosure of it were sudden and abrupt. The fields of the approach held no hint of what was to come. Then, past the gate, the ground fell violently away on every side, grey rocks of an ill shape pierced through it, and the ash trees on the steep slopes overshadowed all. The descent was into silence, without the singing of a bird, into a wizard shade. At the farther end, where the wooded heights retreated somewhat, there was the open space, or circus, of turf; and in the middle of it a very ancient, twisted thorn tree, beneath which the party in the dark had found the little creature that whined and cried out in unknown speech. I turned about, and on my way back I entered the caves, and lit the carriage candle I had brought with me. There was nothing much to see—I never think there is much to see in caves. There was the place where the children and others before them had taken their tea, with a ring of blackened stones within which many fires and twigs had been kindled. In caves or out of caves, townsfolk in the country are always alike in leaving untidy and unseemly litter behind; and here were the usual scraps of greasy paper, daubed with smears of jam and butter, the half-eaten sandwich, and the gnawed crust. Amidst all this nastiness I saw a piece of folded notepaper, and in sheer idleness picked it up and opened it. You have just seen it. When I asked you if you saw anything peculiar about the writing, you said that the letters were rather big and clumsy. The reason of that is that they were written by a child. I don't think you examined the back of the second leaf. Look: 'Rosamund'—Rosamund Brown, that is. And beneath; there, in the corner.

Reynolds looked, and read, and gaped aghast.

'That was—her other name; her name in the dark.'

'Name in the dark?'

'In the dark night of the Sabbath. That pretty girl had caught them all. They were in her hands, those wretched children, like the clay images she made. I found one of those things, hidden in a cleft of the rocks, near the place where they had made their fire. I ground it into dust beneath my feet.'

'And I wonder what her name was?'

'They called her, I think, the Bridegroom and the Bride.'

'Did you ever find out who she was, or where she came from?'

'Very little. Only that she had been a mistress at the Home for Christian Orphans in North Tottenham, where there was a hideous scandal some years before.'

'Then she must have been older than she looked, according to your description.'

'Possibly.'

They sat in silence for a few minutes. Then Reynolds said:

'But I haven't asked you about this formula, or whatever you may call it—all these vowels, here. Is it a cypher?'

'No. But it is really a great curiosity, and it raises some extraordinary questions, which are outside this particular case. To begin with—and I am sure I could go much farther back than my beginning, if I had the necessary scholarship—I once read an English rendering of a Greek manuscript of the second or third century—I won't be certain which. It's a long time since I've seen the thing. The translator and editor of it was of the opinion that it was a Mithraic Ritual; but I have gathered that weightier authorities are strongly inclined to discredit this view. At any rate, it was no doubt an initiation rite into some mystery; possibly it had Gnostic connections; I don't know. But our interest lies in this, that one of the stages or portals, or whatever you call them, consisted almost exactly of that formula you have in your hand. I don't say that the vowels and double vowels are in the same order; I don't think the Greek manuscript has any *aes* or *aas*. But it is perfectly clear that the two documents are of the same kind and have the same purpose. And, advancing a little in time from the Greek manuscript, I don't think it is very surprising that the final operation of an incantation in medieval and later magic consisted of this wailing on vowels arranged in a certain order.

'But here is something that is surprising. A good many years ago I strolled one Sunday morning into a church in Bloomsbury, the headquarters of a highly respectable sect. And in the middle of a very dignified ritual, there rose quite suddenly, without preface or warning, this very sound, a wild wail of vowels. The effect was astounding, anyhow; whether it was terrifying or merely funny, is a matter of taste. You'll have guessed what I heard: they call it 'speaking with tongues', and they believe it to be a heavenly language. And I need scarcely say that they meant very well. But the problem is: how did a congregation of solid Scotch Presbyterians hit upon that queer, ancient and not over-sanctified method of expressing spiritual emotion? It is a singular puzzle.

'And that woman? That is not by any means so difficult. The good Scotchmen—I can't think how they did it—got hold of something that didn't belong to them: she was in her own tradition. And, as they say down there: *asakai dasa*: the darkness is undying.'